D1175379

THE
ETERNAL
QUEST

A Mystical Story of Love

by

JOSEPH WHITFIELD

ᵀᴾ

TREASURE PUBLICATIONS

Roanoke, Virginia 1983

© Joseph Whitfield 1983

All rights reserved

This book, or any parts thereof, may not
be reproduced in any form without prior
written consent of:

TREASURE PUBLICATIONS

P.O. Box 3300

Roanoke, Virginia 24015-1300

Library of Congress Catalog Card Number 82-74371

ISBN 0-912119-00-4

SECOND EDITION - 1989

Manufactured in the United States of America

This book is dedicated to LOVE,
To the understanding of LOVE,
To the act of LOVING,
To all LOVERS,
And to the taming of the power
of LOVE!

Books by **JOSEPH WHITFIELD**

THE TREASURE

OF

EL DORADO

THE ETERNAL QUEST
A Mystical Story of Love

TO DEBI-STARR AND HER SMILE

The most beautiful song I ever heard
    Had no sound —
Its music sprang from your eyes and
    Ignited your face into a smile
Of blissful soundless melodies
    That explodingly
Engulfed my heart and senses
    In a rapture
Of silence song —
    A song of LOVE!

                    Adruum

PREFACE

Voices!

Voices, voices, voices!

Everywhere you go, voices are confronting you, blaring at you, annoying you, attacking you, inflaming you, cajoling you, challenging you, informing you, exhorting you, selling you, lying to you, sweet-talking you, vying for your attention, entertaining you, boring you, appalling you, stupifying you, putting you to sleep, waking you up, hypnotizing you, thrilling you—incessantly. You cannot escape them. You can only try to be selective.

One day I went alone to a quiet place. I desperately needed to get away from all of the discordant voices, noises and distractions of our modern society. I sat in the woods. If you are into meditation, you would say that I sat and meditated.

After drinking in the beautiful silence for a while, I began to realize that it wasn't so silent after all. Gradually, I became aware of the birds, the insects, the breeze through the pine trees. Gradually, I became aware of my own breathing, of a fish splashing in the nearby lake, of a squirrel cracking a nut.

I was rediscovering how much I enjoyed listening to

the true voices of nature, which are in rapport with the flow and harmony of life.

One day while visiting a favorite spot in the woods, I rediscovered another voice. This particular voice was so quiet it was barely perceptible. It came from somewhere deep within my sensory consciousness. It was like a tiny whisper. It was almost too faint to hear it at all. Yet it was unmistakable. I thought, "Is this my imagination?". Whether it was or not, I caught myself straining to listen. After all, I consider myself an expert on voices. I've listened to so many that were boring that I thought I would give this one a chance. It sounded intriguing, if not actually exciting. Also, it was accompanied by an overwhelmingly good feeling that bordered on ecstasy. It was certainly worth a try.

The voice sounded a bit like mine so I was inclined to trust it. The voice told me some things about myself that needed changing for my own good. I knew these things, I just had never done anything about them. The voice told me it was now time to stop procrastinating. It reminded me that if I continued to wait for tomorrow to make needed changes in my life, tomorrow would never come. Tomorrow is only a convenient scapegoat for refusing to face reality today.

That little voice was very convincing. It promised me if I would heed its advice, something very good would come of it. I listened, I heeded and something unusually good came of it.

I hastened back to the woods for more of this intelligent conversation. I listened and listened and listened. I heard the birds, the fish, the squirrels. I heard the insects, the breeze through the pines and my own breathing. I heard a jet airplane fly overhead and I cursed the intrusion.

Then I heard that tiny whisper say, "Does your reaction to that airplane truly express the way you want to be, or are you putting off changing those immature reactions until tomorrow?". What can you say in a situation like that?

I liked the feeling that accompanied the voice. I liked the results that accompanied following its advice. I determined to put a control on my impulsive reactions. I decided that I had discovered a very good thing and I was not going to do anything to jeopardize it.

This communication became a regular and very productive occurrence. I was gradually led, guided and instructed through a series of positive changes in my health, my attitude, my relationships with others, my work habits, my diet and exercise along with my entire approach to life. One must measure the effectiveness of things by the results. The results that I achieved were impressive. I was hooked. If the purpose of that little voice was to win my confidence, it had totally succeeded.

My story could end here, but there is more. It concerns you.

After mastering the process of communicating with that wise little voice, I was subsequently introduced to other inner voices. Some of the things that I have since been told have been incredible. By the standards of the physical world many of these things would be regarded as fantasy. Nevertheless, I am honor bound to relate one particular story to you. I hope you will read it. I know if you do, that you will profit from it. And even if you still regard it as only fantasy, I think you will enjoy it.

CHAPTER 1

On September 21, 1979, a still small voice spoke to me and said, "Hello Joseph, I am Diane. You and I have not spoken before in this lifetime. I am here today with a friend named Michael. With your permission we would like to speak to you."

I replied, "I'm happy to meet you, Diane and Michael. Where are you and what do you wish to speak to me about?"

Diane responded, "Michael and I are no longer in our physical bodies. We live in the mental realms of the Earth. As you know, the mental or astral realms surround the Earth like an aura, and are invisible to most people. Most people in the physical world do not believe that worlds such as ours exist. They have rather nebulous ideas of what happens to you when your physical body dies.

"Michael and I want to tell you an interesting story in the hopes that you will write a book about this experience. Mankind is very much in need of the information that is in our story. Would you consider doing such a thing for us?

"It would have to be an awfully good story, Diane," I replied. "Do you know how much work is involved in writing a book and then trying to get it published?"

"We have observed that it is very difficult, Joseph, but we feel that this story can benefit such a great number of people that it will be well worth the effort. Will you agree to listen to the story before you decide?"

"That's fair enough, Diane," I finally replied. "Do you want to tell me your story now or some other time?"

"Now, please," she said. "Michael will begin the first part."

"We would like to begin our story in the ancient past," Michael began. "Have you ever heard of Cassandra," he asked?

"Yes, I have," I responded. "She was a very beautiful woman who lived in the days of Troy, at the time of the Trojan War."

"That is correct," Michael continued. "Cassandra was one of the daughters of King Priam and Queen Hecuba of Troy. Her beauty was legendary. Perhaps only Helen of Sparta (also known as Helen of Troy) was more renowned as the personification of feminine beauty, grace, charm and perfection. In Cassandra, we have the embodiment of all that a woman can aspire to be. Think of all of the attributes in a woman that can excite the senses and stir the emotions in a man. To gaze upon Cassandra was sufficient to send any man's pulse rate soaring. Indeed, that is what happened. Wherever Cassandra walked, the eyes of men were upon her. And not only the eyes, but the thoughts, for the average man could not gaze upon her without desiring to seduce her, or more happily, be seduced by her. Even the Gods of mythology were not immune to her allure. Apollo, himself, was so captivated by her sensory presence that he made a pact with her to secure her favors."

"Hold on just a minute, Michael," I interrupted. "When

I agreed to give you a few hours of my time to hear your story, it wasn't for the purpose of being entertained with a lesson in mythology! If I want to brush up on mythology, I already have plenty of good books on the subject. I don't need to waste my time in this way."

"Please hear me out, Joseph," Michael replied. "It is not my intent to give you a lesson in mythology. I know it seems ludicrous that I have injected Apollo into my story, but I have a definite purpose in this. Will you permit me to explain?"

"Of course. Go ahead."

"One of the purposes of our story is to bring mythology into a new perspective. You see, mythology has its role in the education, broadening, evolution, enlightenment, entertainment and guidance of man. When understood from a deeper spiritual significance, mythology has done more to elevate mankind than either philosophy or religion."

"You have an interesting point there, Michael," I said. "Now you have raised my curiosity. Please continue."

"Well, as you know," he resumed, "philosophy and religion, like politics and race, have been divisive influences in the growth and evolution of mankind. Mythology on the other hand has been relegated to allegory by most and therefore has not been as controversial. Nevertheless, the greatest thinkers of the ages have always been able to draw great wisdoms from the mythological storehouse. By gleaning allegorical wisdoms from the follies of the Gods, the wisest of men have been able to draw great knowledge. This knowledge has taught wise men how to think. It has taught them about human nature and perhaps even God nature. It has fortified them with the wisdom and understanding to instruct lesser men.

"The wisest of the wise men have always known that the Gods actually do exist, although not exactly as portrayed by mythology or religions. Furthermore, the wisest of the wisest have suspected that the Gods have always cloaked themselves in a few carefully chosen human forms throughout human history. But before I stray too far, let me return to Cassandra and Apollo.

"As I was saying, Apollo made a bargain with Cassandra. In exchange for Apollo's granting to her the gift of prophecy, Cassandra agreed to share her affections with him. Apollo thereupon fulfilled his part of the agreement and bestowed upon Cassandra the ability to foretell the future. Cassandra, for her part, then decided not to keep her end of the agreement. Apollo was understandably furious, for not only was he denied a liaison which he had long sought, but he had granted a gift which even he, a God, could not retract.

"To get even, he moistened the lips of Cassandra with his tongue and ordained that although she would still be able to prophesy, no one would ever believe her. From that day forth no one relied upon her prophecies, much to the sorrow of her time.

"This much about Cassandra has been revealed through mythology. What I am now about to tell you has never been known in history, but is crucial to our story.

"Why did Cassandra refuse to honor her agreement with Apollo? Why did she make such an agreement in the first place? What were the aspirations and goals, the fears and expectations that motivated her life? How did she reach that pinnacle of consummate femininity which made her the object of most men's desires and the envy of women?

"I will answer the last question first. Cassandra's lifetime as Cassandra was the culmination of a hundred lifetimes as a woman. Since I know of your awareness of the reality of reincarnation, I know that you won't have any problem accepting this. Nevertheless, I still wish to make a point so as to avoid later confusion by the readers of this story. Most people have a misconception of what reincarnation means. Many otherwise well-informed people confuse reincarnation with transmigration of the soul. This is a major stumbling block for the average individual in reaching a clearer understanding about the realities of eternal living. Reincarnation is the return of the human soul to a human physical body in a subsequent lifetime, whereas transmigration of the soul is the concept that a human soul might return to the physical world as an animal or fish or some other form of life. This concept is erroneous.

"Now, let's return to Cassandra. Let's briefly trace her evolvement over a span of 91,000 years in the Earth. We'll begin with a lifetime she experienced about 89,000 B.C. in the ancient civilization of Lemuria. Lemuria as you know was an ancient continent in the Pacific Ocean. Only small portions of it remain. Cassandra was born as a daughter to a middle class family of city dwellers. Her father was a skilled craftsman, her mother a homemaker and she was the youngest of four children. The oldest child was a sister and the two middle children were brothers.

"While Cassandra was an old soul in the spiritual realms of life, she never before had had the experience of being in a physical body. So she had a lot to learn. Part of the normal learning experience of being in a physical body is the experience of not remembering your origin before birth. This is also part of the excitement and adventure of a soul's growth. Think for a moment of the sheer drama of entering a new dimension in a new form, and without conscious recall, achieving a lifetime of accomplishment according to a long range plan.

"So this was Cassandra's first lifetime as a physical human being upon a physical world. From the land of spirit she had planned and hoped that this first physical experience would be one of joy and accomplishment. She hoped and prayed that it would set the pattern for the kinds of growth and learning that would most benefit her soul. Although she knew from observation that she would have to experience such things as physical pain for the first time, she thought that she would be able to endure it. She felt that the fun of pleasant physical experiences such as eating, playing, working, dancing and crafts would compensate for any episodes of pain. She was especially looking forward to physical sex. From the realms of spirit, the physical sexual experience appeared compellingly intriguing and inviting.

"This is not to say that the spirit worlds are sexless. It's just that in spirit, sex is expressed differently than in a physical body. In spirit, it's an energy exchange accomplished through total merging of the spirit forms."

"You know, Michael," I said, "I have often wondered about that. I'm sure a lot of others have thought and wondered about it too."

"Well the purpose of this story, Joseph, is not so much to dwell on the spirit side of life's experiences as it is to illustrate the cumulative effect of one's physical incarnations upon the soul's growth and expression.

"Cassandra's name in that first lifetime was Naomi, which means pleasant. Pleasant would be a good description of that first life. Her childhood could be described as normal in that it was filled with the everyday adventure and excitement that accompanies learning and growing in a happy and love-filled environment. Her mother was wise and responsive to her children's needs without being overprotective or neglectful. It was an environment that encouraged creativity and growth and instilled an appreciation of life and of living things. It was certainly close to an ideal setting in which to begin experiencing life in the flesh.

"Her first tentative explorations into the area of physical sex were positive and natural. In the culture in which the family was living, the everyday approach to sex was more enlightened than in your world today. There was no shame to educating your children in all of the natural expressions and purposes of sex. Along with being taught the functions of sex, however, the children were also educated as to the nobility of responsible behavior. This meant that no sexual act should result in the debasement of oneself or another. It also meant that all sexual acts should be accompanied by an attitude of genuine love since it is dealing with one's very life force, and all life force is sacred and is God-connected. A normal pattern of self-stimulation was established at the pubescent stage and started the foundation of physical sexual experience for Cassandra in a physical body.

"During her adolescence, which we will not detail here, Naomi became extremely attracted to the art of dress design along with the craft of weaving fine cloths. In order to pursue these interests, she was apprenticed to one named Aladran, the finest craftsman of refined garments in all of Xanthia, the great city where they lived. One of Aladran's sons, named Ilus, was assigned responsibility to train Naomi in the skills of her chosen craft.

"Naomi proved so proficient as a novice, and she was

so attractive and pleasant to be around, that Ilus' interest
in her rapidly expanded beyond that of a teacher. Within
months their relationship had expanded into an idyllic
personal and intimate relationship. Their expanded bond
was fully sanctioned and applauded by both families as
being a beautiful, healthful and desirable union of two
responsible and talented young people.

"This committment was later formalized into the kind
of marriage that was conventional in that civilization, and
Naomi and Ilus remained together for life. Their life together was strengthened by a high degree of sexual and
emotional compatibility and fulfillment. They were sexually active their entire life. The relationship was completely uninhibited, unselfconscious and natural.

"It was a good start for Cassandra. Not all souls have
such a peaceful and productive first physical incarnation.
However, you must remember that Cassandra was an
old soul in terms of conscious existence in the spiritual
realms. For this reason, she was able to plan her first
Earth life very carefully. She enlisted the aid of many
friends in the spirit worlds to help her while she was in
the physical body. She was also very sensitive or psychic.
Not having been in a physical body before, she had not
accumulated a great dependence upon the physical
senses. Such dependency tends to block out the reality
of extrasensory perceptions. Hence she was frequently
able to receive much valuable assistance on the psychic
level.

"As soon as Naomi left her physical body and returned
to the spirit realms, she began a review of that important
first physical life.

"Thus we begin learning the true drama of Cassandra's
soul growth as a woman. For the next thirteen lifetimes

covering a span of 2,500 years, Cassandra continued to reincarnate and to build experience in the realms of physical living. After four successive lifetimes in Lemuria, she began to experiment with other races, cultures and creeds around the Earth. In the process, she began to build her repertoire of womanhood. She was learning how to be an infant female, a little girl, an adolescent girl, a young woman, a maturing woman, an old woman, a little sister, a big sister, a wife, a mother, a grandmother, an aunt, a cousin, a girl friend, a spinster. She was learning the various skills of the female physical roles. She was learning to be a student, a seamstress, a cook, a companion, a teacher, a healer, a homemaker, a dancer, a craftswoman, etc. She was acquiring the psychological patterns that are normally associated with being female. She was gradually growing more skillful at the art of being a woman in the Earth.

"Between physical lifetimes, she continued to review her soul's progress and growth. She was pleased with herself. She was always surprised after each lifetime to find that she was still 'alive'. It was an interesting game. Before incarnating, she carefully reviewed her previous physical lifetimes and resolved not to repeat her 'mistakes'. Afterwards, when the lifetime was finished, she compared the results with her goals and was usually disappointed at not having achieved all of her desired objectives. Not being able to remember the past was the most frustrating aspect of being physically incarnated. It was like playing cards without a full deck. But that is the way the game is normally played.

"However, the game was not totally one-sided. Each lifetime, she was adding a further accumulation of skills and experiences to the repertoire of her soul. In a literal sense, you might compare one attribute of the soul to the memory bank of a computer. Every single event, every thought, word, deed and feeling that is ever experienced is permanently and automatically recorded within the soul. It is this attribute of the soul which is responsible for producing learned responses while in the physical body. It is this very storehouse which produces what the physical worlds call instinctive behavior. Often such 'instinctive' behavior is nothing more than learned response acquired during previous lifetimes."

"Are you saying that this attribute of the soul is the basic mechanism that is responsible for producing habit patterns in individuals," I asked.

"That's right, Joseph," Michael replied. "At times it produces syndromes which bewilder psychologists and psychiatrists. In fact, one of the main purposes of this story is to dramatize this phenomena by showing its effects upon two souls as they evolve through the physical experience. And speaking of two souls, it's time now for Diane to speak to you."

CHAPTER 2

"Michael is right, Joseph. It's my turn now. We want to keep this story balanced so it will be easier to follow the chain of progression.

"Just as Michael did with Cassandra, I am going to do with Hector. Do you remember Hector?"

"Yes I do, Diane. Like Cassandra, he was also one of the children of King Priam and Queen Hecuba of Troy."

"Well obviously, Joseph, you also recall that Hector was the classic embodiment of manhood. What Cassandra represented as the epitome of feminine perfection, Hector represented in the masculine. There was no man in all of Troy or Greece who was nobler or more brave. In the skills of battle, there was only one man superior to Hector as a warrior. That man was the Greek, Achilles.

"Hector's character and qualities as a husband and as a father were no less admirable than his skill as a warrior. He was handsome and loyal, kind, intelligent and true to his ideals. As a son of the king, he was also a prince of the land. And he was the one prince whom his father, King Priam, relied upon above all the others.

"There seemed to be a very strong energy surrounding Hector. This energy had the same affect upon women that Cassandra's presence exerted over men. For a woman

11

to gaze upon Hector was for that woman to desire to share his bed. Interestingly, men were not jealous of him. He was so respected for his qualities of justice and concern for others that he did not represent a threat to his fellow man, except upon the enemy on the battlefield.

"With all of these attributes, Hector had much to live for. Yet a long life was not to be his destiny. He was slain by the mighty Achilles in a great battle outside the walls of Troy.

"Why did he die so young when he was such a noble example of manhood? For that matter, how had he attained those qualities which set him apart as a man among men and a man desired by women?

"Surely you've guessed the answer, Joseph. Hector's lifetime as Hector was the culmination of a hundred lifetimes as a man. Now, just as Michael did with Cassandra, let's begin to trace Hector's evolvement over the same period of time in the Earth. We can do this because Hector also had his first physical incarnation around 89,000 B.C. in the ancient civilization of Lemuria. To make our story even more interesting, I must tell you that Hector was also born and raised in the great city of Xanthia. I hope you won't think it coincidental if I tell you that he was one of the sons of Aladran. Would it surprise you to learn that he was Ilus?

"Since Michael has already told you of Aladran's reputation as a craftsman, it is obvious that the family enjoyed many advantages in an economic and social way. Yet beyond this, Aladran and his wife were wise and capable parents and they had instilled many fine qualities into their children. Like the parents of Naomi, Ilus' parents had indoctrinated him in an enlightened way concerning the sacredness and responsibility associated with the sexual faculties and their use. In this, Ilus' first incarnation, it was certainly most desirable to form a healthy foundation of sexual habit patterns and practices. In this case, Ilus' pubescent sex life paralleled that of Naomi up to the age of fourteen. His only manner of sexual expression and fulfillment was through masturbation. Yet even this simple act was always entered into reverently as he had been taught by his wise parents.

"At age fourteen, Ilus began an intimate relationship with a lovely thirty year old widow which continued until the time Naomi went to work for his father. Through this relationship Ilus was to learn to balance the physical needs with the emotional and mental needs. It enabled him to mature emotionally and spiritually at a somewhat early age. It also gave him the insight from his own experience to know that a young person can grow rapidly in wisdom and values under the proper guidance and love.

"When he met Naomi, he knew almost immediately that she was that special someone for him. Thanks to his unique relationship with the lovely widow, he knew what characteristics he desired in a wife and companion. Soon, there was no doubt in his mind that Naomi fulfilled these criteria.

"Ilus had preceded Naomi into the Earth by ten years. This had allowed him sufficient time to become a skilled craftsman and an emotionally mature young man prior to Naomi's apprenticeship. You see, they were friends in the realms of spirit before they came to Earth, and they had planned to be together during that important first incarnation. Their plan had worked. Such prearrangements frequently do not work, because plans are flexible and often change after incarnating.

"Thus we begin the odyssey of Cassandra and Hector in the Earth 91,000 years ago. In Hector's case, as contrasted to Cassandra, there was to be a striving to master all of the attributes of manhood. Hector and Cassandra knew in advance that such a quest was long and arduous. But they also knew that this experience was absolutely necessary in the progression of the soul's growth. Eventually, all souls must undergo the physical evolvement. For a soul to delay this experience in no way cancels the obligation, but merely postpones the inevitable.

"Wherein Cassandra was beginning to build her repertoire of female skills and memories, Hector would be concentrating his attention on the mastery of male characteristics and experiences. So we find Hector busily learning how to be an infant male, a little boy, an adolescent boy, a young man, a maturing man, an old man, a little brother, a big brother, a husband, a father, a grandfather, an uncle, a cousin, a boy friend, a bachelor. He was to acquire the various skills of the male physical roles. His preadolescent childhoods were to be spent doing little boy things familiar to the races, religions and cultures into which he incarnated. The adolescent years of his many lives would likewise be spent in various boyhood pursuits that distinguish boyhood from manhood. His goal was to inculcate himself thoroughly in all of those attributes which are favorably looked upon as denoting virility and manliness. He would fill those soul memory banks connected with physical lives with a total programming of manhood as practiced in all of the various civilizations into which he would incarnate.

"In the next three thousand years, Hector incarnated fifteen times. Like Cassandra, the next four Earth lives were spent in Lemuria. Except for that first lifetime, however, they were not to spend any future lives as husband

and wife. This is not to say that they were never together again in the Earth. They were frequently together as relatives and friends and as mere acquaintances, but they were never again to share the total intimacy of marriage until their final Earth lifetime. In this connection, I think it is relevant to note that in each life in which they were connected in any way, there was always an 'instinctive' recognition of each other.

"As is customary and necessary after each lifetime, Hector examined his preceding Earth life very carefully. He noted that he was making progress toward his goal. He made an important decision at this point. Having experienced fifteen incarnations in the span of three thousand years, he decided to spend a longer time in the worlds of spirit before continuing his evolution in the physical worlds.

"Cassandra concurred in this decision. She felt the same way herself. After thirteen lifetimes in the Earth she believed that a prolonged period of assimilation and rest was required.

"The Earth in those years was different in many ways than is revealed in your presently recorded history. For example, the geographical land masses. Lemuria was part of a continent which is now mostly submerged in the Pacific Ocean. Hawaii is one of its few remaining fragments. Also, there was a large land mass in the Atlantic Ocean which was later to contain a great civilization known to you as Atlantis. While Lemuria itself was in many respects well advanced in technology and the arts and sciences, most of the Earth was relatively primitive. Several of Cassandra's and Hector's incarnations had been spent in various of the primitive societies in other parts of the Earth. A few of these lives had been quite difficult and traumatic. A rest was needed.

CHAPTER 3

"It is necessary to the continuity of our story, Joseph, to now mention something about the time in between Earth incarnations that is spent in the spirit worlds. We think it is also necessary for some description to be made of these worlds in our story.

"In the first place, there is not just one 'place' where people go when they leave their physical bodies. There are many possibilities. For instance, each planet has an area around and above the surface that is like an aura. This area contains those levels of the spirit worlds that are sometimes referred to as the astral or mental realms. After the death of the physical body, all souls must pass into this area. Most souls remain here as they continue their evolution, until their next physical incarnation. But keep in mind that there are various levels or vibrations in the mental realms. Some of these levels are quite low. They would correspond to some of the most debased levels in the physical world. In like manner, some levels of the mental worlds are exceedingly high and are like 'heaven' in many respects. Souls in these realms quite naturally gravitate to the level which most closely matches their consciousness or their need to experience.

"Now, besides the astral or mental realms, there are

the true spiritual realms. These spiritual realms may or may not be connected with a planet. They represent a vibration which is beyond that of the mental or the physical realms. It is the spiritual realms which constitute that experience referred to as heaven. Just as with the mental realms, there are varying levels or vibrations in these heavenly kingdoms. Beyond the spiritual kingdoms there is the true paradise which is yet to come to those who are deserving. We are not qualified to speak of paradise, since we have only recently learned of its existence. In fact, to our knowledge no one is qualified to speak of it with the lone exception of the Great Archangel Michael. And the Great Michael does not speak of it. Perhaps the reason he does not is because God called him there and he has not yet returned. Everyone in the spiritual and mental worlds awaits his return so that we may learn more about it.

"The Great Michael has told those of us in the mental and spiritual realms many interesting things. Some of these things had never before been known in any realm or kingdom. We have been given permission to relay these things to you. Perhaps the most startling information ever released to the souls of all realms concerns the evolutionary process of the soul itself. Here is what Archangel Michael has told us concerning this:

'All too long, those who teach of God have taught the worlds the evolutionary process of the soul as if the soul must advance itself from the physical body to the mind and then to the spirit. But this has never been God's way, and all who have sought God have misunderstood God's plan but for only a handful and a few. The Earth is God's key world that He has chosen. But understand, the evolutionary process is from God to the Earth. All living things must advance from the soul and the spiritual realm, and then into the mental realms. And in all of the things that they learn from these realms and these worlds, the last step would be to the physical worlds. The flow of God's life, and there is nothing but God's life and living; out from God and then from all things to return to God. Then, in the final release, once more into the physical. God is as a mighty wave sent out from Himself, and then recalled and then sent out once more, never to recall again. The Eternals are the first of God's latter day processes, of those who will leave God, and become like God.'

"All souls in the mental and spiritual worlds were startled when the Great Michael first revealed this information to us. It had been universally believed until that time that the evolutionary process began in the physical body and progressed to the mental realms and then to the spiritual realms. It was very ego-shattering to many of those in the spiritual worlds, for it was about that time that the Great Michael also revealed the existence of Paradise beyond the Great Blue Wall. Those in Heaven (the spiritual or etheric or Christ worlds) had mistakenly believed up until that time that Heaven was the highest evolvement that any soul could hope to attain. For them to learn after countless eons of time that there was yet a higher world, provided a much-needed lesson in humility for us one and all! Up until the time of this revelation, many souls in Heaven had exhibited a great deal of pride. They had looked down upon those in the mental realms and those in physical bodies. There were many in spirit who never intended to venture into these 'lower worlds.' Imagine the shock which they must have experienced when they learned for the first time from the Great Michael that they, too, would eventually have to complete this evolutionary process.

"The information was even more shocking in another sense for many. The fact is that the majority of those in spirit did not actually believe in the existence of God as a Being, as an entity. It is true that there had always been references to God. These references were, however, deemed to signify an impersonal creative force rather than a viable, personal, individualized intelligent being. Archangel Michael had always referred to God in a personal way, but since none other than the Great Michael had ever seen God, we suppose it is only natural that most strong ego-centered souls soon refused to accept the reality literally. We have all since learned better!

"Perhaps equally startling was the story the Great Michael told us concerning the Eternals. There had long been whisperings in Heaven and the mental realms about God-like beings called the Eternals. In many respects the stories were similar to the mythology of the Gods in the Earth. Because they were considered by most to be mythological in origin, few took the stories seriously or literally. The Great Michael's revelation to us of God's Divine Plan removed all skepticism and replaced it with profound awe and joy. We tell you about all of these things, Joseph, because they have the deepest of connections to the rest of our story. We would now like to tell you the story of the Eternals as we in Heaven and the mental realms heard it from the Great Michael.

'Beloved ones. It is I, your brother Michael, speaking. What I have come to tell you has been whispered since the beginning, but has never been clearly known or understood before now. It is the story of the meaning and purpose of God's Divine Plan.

'It was never in sequence for this information to be presented in this way until this time. To have done so would have run the risk of intentional or unintentional interference by those who were either obstructive or overzealous in their approach to life and to God.

'Who would dare dream that God, in His greatness, was actually alone? Who would dare imagine that God in His supremacy yearned for one friend to say "I care"? Who could fathom God's need for an unselfish "thank you"? Who would know, for who could know how human God actually is? Who could fathom that God's needs are as great as His desires for you and your happiness? God has a need of a love as pure as His own as for you, and all life denied Him this most. And He contemplated the problem— His greatness was the problem–His supremacy was the problem; so great that He could not undermine Himself in any way but by giving, and giving, and giving and giving—until He had no more to give, but giving still. And in this process, God lost the will to live, for He was alone.

'Can any of you, my beloved ones, possibly begin to understand what it must be like to be all-knowing, all-powerful, yet all alone? Can you not realize that even in your worlds that those among you who are truly great, are isolated by that greatness, and are alone and crave and need love and companionship? But at least they have God's love. How much greater then is the aloneness and isolation of our God, the God who made it all?

'For an eternity unto an eternity, God contemplated the problem and searched for the solution to end His loneliness.

'Finally, God reasoned that He could not end His isolation other than by lessening Himself. By this, He reasoned that it would be necessary to literally separate Himself into distinct divisions or attributes.

'Only by this division of Himself could God ensure the perpetuation of those inherent qualities and characteristics necessary and vital to the fulfillment of His needs. Having reached this point in His reasoning, God undertook to formulate a plan whereby the success of His experiment would be assured.

'In His all-knowingness, God knew that He would never be happy unless and until He had the companionship of Gods like unto Himself. Without having experienced these things before, God reasoned the need for a race of Gods. Amongst them, these Gods must manifest the attributes that He Himself possessed. Then God foresaw the kinds and types of relationships that would be most conducive to ending loneliness, boredom and pain, and producing pleasure, companionship, adventure, discovery, bliss and fulfillment.

'Having now foreseen His needs and the method of filling those needs, God proceeded in the creation of a race of new Gods. He did this by dividing His own being and substance into twelve divisions or attributes, naming these new God-Beings ETER-NALS, and giving each ETERNAL a name.

'For an age unto an age, all was glorious in the land the Gods call Paradise. God had succeeded in putting an end to His loneliness and all was perfect.

'That was the problem. All was perfect. All was predictable. The excitement of discovery, adventure and surprise was missing. The old boredom was gone, it was true, but a new boredom had taken its place. Each of the Gods knew all there was to know about the other in a genetic sense. Having been created equally and simultaneously by the Primal God, They really had no secrets from each other, nor from the Primal God. All was too predictable, all was known. A plan must now be devised to end this boredom forever.

'So God called unto His side His first ETERNAL, Adruum, and asked of him, "What would you be willing to do for Me, Adruum, to prove your love for Me?". "Why do You ask this of me, O God, for You already know that I love You with my whole heart and soul, with my whole mind and emotions, and that I would do anything without hesitation to bring a smile to Your lips, a song to Your ears, joy to Your heart?" This response in itself brought a smile to the Great God's lips and He said to Adruum, "We must put an end to the boredom or our predictability. We must create a solution that will impart to each ETERNAL a uniqueness that will forever dispel the boredom of our prescience, each for the other."

'And Adruum responded, "And how may I help to accomplish this, O God? In what way may I serve You to ensure that Your joy will be complete?" The Great God looked at His most beloved ETERNAL for a long time before He replied, "I have formulated a new plan, Adruum. Though it brings sadness to me, I know in My heart that it is the only solution to our needs. I must send you on a journey and a mission beyond the Great Blue Wall, out into the endless void. Your journey will last for an eternity unto an eternity. In the endless time of your mission, you will forget all about your identity, about who you are and what you mean to Me. But in the process of your mission, you will amass such knowledge, wisdom, experience, variety, adventure, pain, loneliness, isolation, discovery, suffering, joy, creativity and self-mastery that you will never again be predictable, even to Me. In this process, you will also learn what it means to be a God. You will learn the total discipline required in order for you to be entrusted with the power of God, a power so formidable, so great and absolute, that one single unguarded thought could destroy all of the known worlds. Following you, I shall send out the remaining ETERNALS, one by one, but you are to be the first."

'Adruum so loved God that it never entered his consciousness to refuse. Adruum was known as the ETERNAL of Love. Love was his primary attribute. Adruum hastened to the side of the second ETERNAL, Epsilon. Epsilon was the twin soul of Adruum. She was his counterpart, his beloved. Next to the Primal God, Adruum loved Epsilon above all others.

With great sadness, Adruum told Epsilon of the mission that God had asked of him, a mission that would separate them virtually forever. They embraced each other in a fusion of total love and cried the cry of anguish that only such a separation can induce.

'Adruum then bade each of the other ETERNALS farewell and stepped beyond the Great Blue Wall into the great void. Since no ETERNAL had ever before ventured into the void, neither Adruum nor the other ETERNALS knew what awaited him. In that moment, none of the other ETERNALS yet knew that they were in turn to follow. None that is, except Epsilon. Epsilon had known in her heart from the moment that Adruum had told her of the mission that she would soon follow in search of her beloved. So perceptive was Epsilon to the needs of her beloved, that when she heard the whisper of Adruum in her soul saying 'I need you,' she stepped into the void to begin the almost endless search for him.

'The scriptures of many worlds and of many religions carry this story in one form or another, though it has never been correctly interpreted by anyone before this time. I deliberately interpret it for you now.

'In one of the many scriptures of God's chosen key world, the Earth, in the first book dictated to Moses, the book of Genesis, we find an account of this unprecedented event. In Genesis, the meaning of the allegorical symbolisms is this. To eat of the fruit of the tree of knowledge is absolutely necessary to gain the knowledge and wisdom of Godhood. To eat of this fruit, however, means to forfeit the bliss of Paradise in pursuit of this knowledge. It means that the allegorical Adam and Eve knew that in order to fulfill God's Divine Plan, they would be required to forsake Paradise in pursuit of the knowledge that is essential to Godhood. Adam and Eve were Adruum and Epsilon, the first ETERNALS to leave Paradise on a quest for God—THE ETERNAL QUEST!

'Furthermore, Adam and Eve are symbolic of God himself. The taking of a rib from Adam to form the counterpart, Eve, symbolizes God lessening Himself by taking from His own substance to create the ETERNALS, and thence all life.

'The sending out of Adam (Adruum) characterizes the male (idea) principle of God going forth into the unknown to ideate the needs of a creation to fulfill the plan. The sending out of Eve (Epsilon) characterizes the female (creative) principle of God going forth into the unknown to create or give birth to the ideas of the positive male principle.

'So what Genesis and other scriptures are telling you in a hidden way is that in order for the creation to come into being, it was necessary for God to separate into the male-female, positive-negative principles or polarities. The interaction and separation of these opposite, but complimentary aspects of God, was essential for the ideation-creation to occur. And by that same token the ideation-creation was essential to provide the fertile training ground for the new race of Gods, mankind. Mankind is God's greatest idea-creation. God is the man of yesterday, man is the God of tomorrow, though he still sleeps.'"

"What a bewilderingly beautiful story, Diane!" I exclaimed. "Please, let's pause for a while. I want to digest what you have just told me. I don't want any other thoughts to intrude right now."

"Certainly, Joseph," Diane replied. "Just signal when you're ready to resume."

I must confess, this story of the Great Archangel Michael was having an enormous impact upon me. I reflected for quite some time before I allowed Diane to continue. Finally, I told her to proceed.

"It's interesting that you asked me to pause when you did, Joseph. It was at that same point that the Great Michael stopped speaking when he told us the story. At that time, not one voice was raised to so much as ask a question. All waited, for they sensed that more was to come. Finally, the Great Michael spoke again.

'What I am saying, my beloved ones, is obvious. Our God had become a duality, a Mother God and a Father God. In order for this duality to function in behalf of the Divine Plan, it was necessary for an actual separation to take place. This separation was required for the necessity of safeguarding Paradise as well as to ensure the formation of the Creation.

'You will remember that beyond Paradise there was only the void. It was in the void that Mother God would fashion and give birth to the Creation. And it was the Creation that was to be the testing ground and classroom for molding the Godling ETERNALS into the fruition for their responsibilities as Gods.

'Following Adruum and Epsilon, the other ETER-NALS made their way into the void. They did not all leave Paradise willingly, but in the end they realized that it truly was not a matter of choice.

'I, myself, was the last to leave. It was not an unwillingness that held me back, but obedience to my God. You see, I too am one of the ETERNALS. Our God had need for one of His ETERNALS to be His liaison between the Creation and Paradise.

'I cannot begin to tell you the countless ages that have passed since the Plan began. During all of this time, our Father God and our Mother God have been separated and lonely. They would not allow Themselves the pleasure which was denied to Their beloved children. They would patiently wait until the end of time for Their reunion. They would wait until the success of Their Divine Plan was assured. They would endure what no one else could endure, but They had no choice for that is what it means to be God.

'When I left Paradise I created the Citadel, which was the Heaven originally referred to in many Holy Books throughout the many worlds. Many of you who hear me now were with me then. It was believed by most that it was the highest level to which a soul could aspire. They were wrong. I let them continue in this mistaken belief for lessons of their own ego.

'Later, the vibration that characterized the Citadel was expanded so as, in effect, to produce many 'Heavens' throughout the Creation. This was necessary to accommodate the countless souls that were proliferating throughout the Creation.

'This proliferation was proof of the activity of the ETERNALS. You must understand that the ETERNALS are enormous beings the size of galaxies. Billions of souls are but fragmentations of the ETERNALS. Human beings are these individualized expressions gaining experience in countless worlds and situations.

'Many of you have heard one or more of the names by which the ETERNALS have been known, but you did not realize who they actually were—names such as Jehovah, Elohim, Lam, Nelphi, Prelude, Logos, Tashmel, Elder, Reme, Saji, Yahweh and my name, Michael. Most of these ETERNALS have one or more human embodiments in the Earth today, including the Primal God. Someday these major identities will be revealed to a disbelieving mankind.

'Before I leave, I want to speak of Good and Evil. Good and Evil exist as a barometer for measuring your spiritual growth. Evil is not an invention of a malevolent God, nor is Good provided as proof of God's kindness. Both are necessary to ensure that each and every soul will someday learn that Love is the only reason to live at all. As a soul truly learns the lesson of Love, that soul automatically rises above both Good and Evil, and will never again suffer the feeling of the loss of Love.'

"Needless to say, Joseph," Diane continued, "The Great Michael's revelations had a most profound effect upon all realms. Most of you in the physical body do not realize it, of course, but in the realms of mind and of spirit, we too have schools and philosophies and dogmas and concepts concerning the nature of God and man. No school or philosophy or dogma or concept has remained unaffected since the Great Michael spoke.

"As for Michael and me, it has helped us to appreciate even more the sacrifices we have made in our efforts to evolve. It has helped us to appreciate even more our responsibility to share with others the painful lessons we have learned.

"More than anything else, it was the Great Michael's story that persuaded Michael and me to reach out to you and share our story in the hope that it would benefit man in the Earth."

CHAPTER 4

"Since Diane and I have a definite sequence to follow in relating our story to you, Joseph, I will take over at this point for a while," Michael interjected.

"Welcome back, Michael," I said. "Please speak."

"Following Hector's fifteen incarnations in the Earth, Cassandra and Hector had a long consultation concerning their goals and progress. Since they had originally planned to assist each other as much as possible in mastering the physical dimension, they felt it was now necessary to make a thorough evaluation of their efforts. They both agreed that a long rest was needed. The mental realms where they resided were very beautiful and pleasant. They could experience a high level of fulfillment in this setting.

"From the point of view of Earth time, over twenty thousand years passed before Cassandra's next incarnation. That is a very long time from your perspective. From the perspective of the mental realms, it does not have the same significance. Time is based on motion. The motion of one body relative to another body creates time. By this very definition you can plainly see therefore that time only applies to the physical worlds. It does not exist here or in the spiritual realms. An age or an epoch in your world may be just a seeming moment here.

"When Cassandra finally decided that she had rested sufficiently, she again conferred with Hector regarding their next series of incarnations in the Earth. During the twenty thousand year Earth time span since their last incarnation, they observed that the civilization of Lemuria had declined to a mere remnant of its ancient glory. They consulted with the wise ones of the mental realms who maintained the records and projections of events in the physical Earth to learn what they could about what could be expected to occur there. They learned that the birth of a new and great civilization was taking place. Granted it would take many thousands of years, but it would be exciting to participate in its infancy. And so it was that Cassandra took another physical body in the early stages of the establishment of the civilization of Atlantis."

"Pardon my interruption, Michael. But are you sure that you want information concerning Atlantis to be included in your story?"

"We consider it necessary and pertinent to keep our story just as authentic as possible, Joseph."

"Well frankly, Michael, I don't have any problem with either Lemuria or Atlantis insofar as my beliefs are concerned. However, I'm trying to keep it in mind that you want me to write your story for other people. The truth is that very few people in this world believe in these tales about ancient unrecorded civilizations. They are universally believed to be pure fantasy, just figments of over-imaginative writers' minds."

"We do understand that, Joseph. A major part of the difficulty of mastering the physical worlds lies in the fact that people always require proof of a physical nature rather than making the effort to develope their psychic capabilities. But that's all right. Remember, if we keep the story interesting enough for people to read it, they don't have to believe it. Most of them will get the point anyway. I'll mention in passing though that physical evidence will soon be uncovered in the Earth to prove the past existence of both ancient civilizations!

"Let me continue. There were no large cities of real consequence in the Earth at that time. What was to become Poseid, the great metropolis of Atlantis, was then a large village on the western shore of the continent in what is now called the Atlantic Ocean. Poseid was not very far from what is now the State of Florida in the United States. It was here that Cassandra decided to spend the first in her new series of lifetimes.

"Before I proceed with the telling of this particular lifetime, now would be a good time to inform you of some very interesting facts concerning some of the preparations necessary for an important incarnation. I have already mentioned to you about the agreements entered into with others in the realms of spirit and mind prior to incarnation. These agreements form the basis of a coordinated plan whereby many things can be accomplished for an individual's soul growth, for the Earth's advancement and for the continued progress of the Divine Plan.

"First of all, the incarnating soul decides the game plan. The more important the lifetime is to be, the greater care is used in formulating the goals and objectives to be accomplished. Everything must be planned and coordinated with relation to its cause and effect upon everything else. This is no easy task. Whatever we do in life, whatever decisions we make, affects a great many other lives and situations. Having established one's goals and objectives, therefore, one proceeds to the selection of parents, relatives, friends, culture, race, religion, intelligence factors, bodily characteristics, etc., that will be required to insure success.

"Having selected one's parents, one then proceeds with the task of influencing the occurrence of a sexual union at the most propitious time to accomplish fertilization. From the point of view of eternal living, I must tell you that it is not important to us whether or not the parental couple is married according to Earth standards and cultures. What is important to us is that the parental requisites are conducive to all of the factors required of our incoming souls.

"The timing of one's birth in accordance with the positioning of planetary influences is vitally important. The sex of the child is important. The physical characteristics are important, along with the general health endurance factors. The physiological configurations that determine to a degree the mental potential are important. The psychological configurations that will influence the personality characteristics are important. Truly, everything is important. That is why so little is left to chance.

"It is time for Earth parents to more fully understand that they are only custodians of the incoming infant. In most instances, everything about the infant, including the infant's name, has been influenced by the soul who then becomes the infant.

"Oftentimes, a tremendous amount of genetic engineering is performed by the incoming soul. Do you think it is by chance, or by 'an act of God' that there is often such a great difference between so many parents and their offspring? It is seldom either, I assure you! After conception has occurred, the incoming soul usually has a great deal of influence upon the proper development of the fetus. The craving of certain foods that is so commonplace with expectant mothers, for instance, can be influenced to provide certain vitamins or minerals or other nutrients that are essential to the desired genetic blueprint.

"Someday soon, Earth parents will play a far more conscious role in this process. What a happy day that will be.

"So, on March 10, 65,937 B.C., a precious little girl named Cyntha was born in a thriving village by the sea. Someday that village would be the greatest city of the greatest civilization in the Earth. Someday that little girl would be the most beautiful and sought after of women in still another civilization to come.

"Cyntha was the first and only child of a wonderful young couple. This parental arrangement had been agreed upon while the young parents were still in the mental realms. Furthermore, Cassandra had been assisting them from the mental realms ever since they themselves had incarnated. The father's name was Byrten, the mother, Rhea.

"As you can appreciate, life in that day and setting was not so structured as it would be in a more mature civilization. Byrten provided for the little family by working as a carpenter for a builder of boats. Rhea, for her part, was daily becoming more skilled at the art of hand weaving crude cloths. You must understand that neither Byrten nor Rhea worked in a formal way. They worked in a way that was natural to the level of their culture. That is, they worked when there was work to be done, when work was available and when it fulfilled their creative or sustenant needs.

"In this form of culture one developed their inherent skills as much as possible and then bartered their skill for whatever needs they could fulfill in this way. The skill of a carpenter and a weaver were both basic to any culture. At this stage of Atlantis' birth, whoever possessed such skills would thrive.

"Thus Cyntha entered into the new Atlantis into an environment that was to maximize her evolvement as a physical human being, as a woman.

"As an infant and as a growing little girl, Cyntha was the beneficiary of much attention, much love and patient guidance. Before she could walk, it was already obvious that she took an unusual interest in Rhea's weaving. This made Rhea happy. Not only did she now have someone she dearly loved as a constant companion to share the interests of her vocation, but it also simplified looking after the child as well. When Cyntha was but a few years old, she was already beginning to teach herself the art of handweaving. With Rhea's guidance she soon grew very skillful. By the time she reached puberty, she began having dreams and visions of a machine, an apparatus, that would enable one to weave much finer cloths. At this stage of the new Atlantean culture, there was no such machine. All weaving was done by the arduous process of intertwining course fibers by hand.

"As you have probably surmised, Joseph, it was part of Cyntha's life plan to re-invent the loom in the Earth. You will recall that in Cassandra's first incarnation, as Naomi, she had become a highly skilled craftswoman under the tutelage of Aladran and Ilus. She had been so skilled in that life that she could actually build a loom. In fact, she had invented refinements that substantially improved the machine at that time.

"Whenever a dream or a vision of the loom would occur, Cyntha would enthusiastically relate the details to Rhea. Finally, one day when Cyntha and Rhea were sharing the idea of the loom with Byrten, Byrten leaped excitedly to his feet and declared, 'Let's build such a machine. After all, am I not a skilled carpenter?'.

"Thus was begun a long and tedious process of trial and error which lasted for fourteen frustrating years. You realize, of course, that there were no papers and pens or pencils to sketch and plan with. Mostly there was just the ground to sketch out an idea of the vision. But patience, coupled with destiny and Cyntha's confidence in her vision, finally produced the first very crude, but workable loom in an age. Byrten must also receive a large share of the credit in this tremendous achievement. I must tell you. Byrten was also one of the sons of Aladran. His name in that life was Virga. In his life as Virga, it had been his responsibility to construct and maintain all of the mechanical equipment of Aladran. He was a highly skilled carpenter then as well as an inventor of some repute. He had worked with Naomi to produce the refinements in the loom that Naomi had developed.

"So you see, in the process of tracing a soul's development and growth through a series of incarnations, we begin to see a pattern express itself here. Any learned skill becomes a permanent part of the repertoire of the soul. At any subsequent time, such skills can be rapidly redeveloped if they are consistent with the soul's growth and plans.

"The importance of Cyntha's rediscovery of the loom could in no way be exaggerated. Its significance would rapidly begin to transform an ordinary village into the first stages of an economic crossroads of the world. Let us briefly follow this development.

"As soon as the first loom became functional, both Cyntha and Rhea became skilled in its use. The quality of the cloth which was produced was far superior to any thing else in the known world. Demand for such cloth spread very rapidly and brought much success at the bartering tables for the little family. Soon Byrten constructed another loom while Rhea taught an apprentice how to use it. Within a few years the demand for their product was bringing traffic to the village of Poseid from far and wide. This increased demand was met with the construction of still more looms and more apprentices becoming skilled weavers. The inventiveness of Cyntha, accompanied by the enthusiasm and support of both Rhea and Byrten, produced ever finer and more beautiful cloths until the family became very wealthy and famous by the standards of that culture.

"Such economic successes produce a power of attraction which in turn creates more success. This spreads to the surrounding communities by the law of multiplication and a chain reaction occurs which can ignite a world.

"You mustn't get the idea that all that Cyntha ever did was to work. There was ample time in her life for other pursuits. Little Poseid's culture allowed such diversions which we would describe as folk dancing, various kinds of feasts during the year and sexual freedom before pairing. There was no formal schooling as such at this point and no written language yet. From an early age, Cyntha mixed freely with her peers and was highly regarded as a playmate, companion and friend.

"She had strong sexual drives which she frequently indulged with herself and with young men and she was very happy most of the time. As she progressed in her adolescence her sex life was sublimated to a degree because of the amount of time and effort spent inventing the loom. This sublimation was later compensated for by her marriage to an outstanding young man named Themis, son of the boat builder.

"Although Themis had lived in Lemuria during the time of Naomi, they were only casual acquaintances then. Themis had been a sea captain who transported raw silk threads and yarns to Aladran from which was spun the treasured silk cloths. She had seen him a number of times over the years, but they had never developed a friendship, only a mutual respect. The noteworthy fact that I wish to record here is that Themis, too, had a strong sex drive. In Cyntha he found a very willing, imaginative and active lover. They were harmonius and compatible and they missed no opportunity or method of fulfilling themselves with each other.

"After having spent thirteen and nineteen lifetimes respectively in the physical body, Cyntha and Themis clearly had already developed strong leanings from the sexual habit patterns etched into their souls. So at this point you could say with some validity, they were doing what comes naturally. That is to say, the habit patterns of the sexual expression in the physical body were becoming well established and predictable. The process of repeated behavior patterns over a period of a number of lifetimes was already producing 'instinctive' behavior in a number of areas of their sex lives.

"Cyntha and Themis lived to the ages of 96 and 97. They had three children, eleven grandchildren and many great grandchildren. The enterprise begun in this life flourished as a family business for over three hundred years. Both the enterprise and the family grouping provided a splendid vehicle for friends in the mental realms to incarnate into.

"There is much more to tell about Cyntha, but it cannot

be included in this story. If we tell too much about each life of Cassandra and Hector, not only will our story be too long, but we fear it will lose some of its impact. I'll now let Diane continue with Hector's next incarnation."

CHAPTER 5

"Hi, Joseph. It's me again," said Diane.

"I must admit, Diane," I replied, "I am finding your story fascinating. I hope that when I get around to writing it that it will be equally spellbinding to those who read it. In the beginning, you and Michael said that if I had any questions as we went along to ask them. I'd like to ask you how long mankind has been incarnating in the Earth?"

"For over two hundred million years, Joseph," Diane informed me.

"Did Cassandra and Hector incarnate within that span of time?"

"Not in the Earth," Diane responded. "They lived only in the mental and spiritual realms before incarnating into Lemuria."

"I'm curious as to why you keep mentioning Cassandra's and Hector's sex life in each incarnation," I said. "You really don't say much about it, but you do make a point of mentioning it."

"We want to document the formation of soul engrams that will have a profound bearing on their future Earth lifetimes," Diane said.

"Thank you," I said. "I have no further questions at this time."

"Then I'll bring you up to date on Hector," Diane continued. "Hector did not incarnate during Cassandra's lifetime as Cyntha. He remained behind in the mental realms to observe and assist where possible. From his observations and consultations with the wise ones who maintain the records and projections of events in the Earth, Hector knew that Poseid's prosperity was beginning to stir the greed of those bent on conquest and power.

"News of the village which had grown into a town and then into a thriving city in a few generations was bound to attract those who would rather live off of the sweat of others than work. Hector foresaw that within a generation, a serious military threat would be raised against Poseid by jealous neighboring communities. It was important to the Divine Plan to protect the family, the culture and the enterprises that had grown up around Cyntha during her lifetime.

"Hector decided that his next lifetime needed to be in Poseid in the Cyntha family business. He made preparations accordingly. He would see to it that he would become interested in military defense during that lifetime. He gained the promise of cooperation from friends with great skill in combat to inspire him from the mental realms. Cassandra pledged her aid in rallying all of the family and friends in Poseid to look to Hector for leadership. In this, Hector's sixteenth incarnation, there would be the foundation of a great new skill—that of a warrior.

"His parents were carefully chosen by Hector. The best combination to produce the needed qualities of body, mind and temperament were decided upon. The fetus was manipulated with great skill to guarantee physical endurance, dexterity, strength and coordination. The more subtle manipulations required to influence courage, sagacity and tenacity were also attended to.

"Hector became a great grandson of Cyntha, born the year following her death. He was the first born and only son of Theseus and Hilda. He was named Victor. He later had two younger sisters called Minerva and Iris. As we shall see, this one, loving, close-knit family unit was almost singularly responsible for saving Poseid.

"The childhood of these children was distinguished by a number of qualities, attributes and events. They were each physically attractive and very active. From the beginning they displayed a strong devotion to each other as well as towards their parents. Perhaps it was this devotion that also made them extremely perceptive to each other's needs. It was soon evident that their bright-eyed curiosity bespoke of a high level of intelligence as well.

"Because of their love for each other, they normally included each other in their games with other children. This, in spite of age differences. Furthermore, because of their strong leadership qualities, a voice of objection was seldom raised by any of the other children.

"It was readily apparent to anyone who might have observed, that they often showed signs of speaking to or otherwise communicating with 'imaginary' beings. As you know, this is typical of many children. As you also know, many times the 'imaginary' beings are real—just as real as our communication at this very moment. Too often, parents foolishly scold their children when they observe this behavior, and in the process they cripple a very valuable talent. Not so the parents of Victor, Minerva and Iris. Their parents knew what was taking place, for they themselves had well-developed gifts of what you call extra-sensory perception.

"Usually, the games that most interested Victor were war type games. Although no one in the city was aware of what war was, there never having been one in Poseid, a minor level of crime had given rise as the village had grown into a city. Awareness of this crime had instilled into many the necessity of preparedness and self-defense. This growth had also given rise to the necessity of a rudimentary form of municipal government. I will not go into detail here except to say that no strong leadership on a governing level had yet developed.

"In the little 'war' games that Victor and the other children played, Victor was always the leader. Victor did not always lead the 'good guys,' but he always controlled the play. Whether he was the 'good guy' or the 'bad guy,' his side always won. During the games, he would frequently consult with Minerva or Iris. No one ever knew just exactly what it was that they consulted about, and though the other children would often ask, they were never given an answer. What they were doing was exchanging information and impressions received from their 'unseen' friends. What was happening was that these innocent childhood games were preparing them for a difficult role ahead!

"As these beautiful children grew into adolescence, their father, Theseus, was chosen by the other family members to head the flourishing family enterprises. The business through the years had grown to include shipping, fishing, farming and the manufacture of carts as well as ownership of the principle marketplace in Poseid. The marketplace occupied a choice location near the center of the city, close to the waterfront and easily accessible from everywhere.

"Theseus was well-prepared for this responsibility. He was familiar with every aspect of the various facets of the family enterprises. He was wise and fair in his handling of people. He was astute and knowledgeable in the handling of business matters.

"The children were very interested in the family business. Adolescence was diminishing their preoccupation with childhood games. They saw in commerce and the crafts many opportunities to satisfy their sense of curiosity, adventure, achievement and growth. Theseus and Hilda were both very pleased at this interest.

"At the age of twelve, Victor was allowed to assist in one of the family stalls in the marketplace. His job was to keep the area spotlessly clean and to help keep the merchandise neatly displayed. Sometimes he would run errands. After a few months he became quite bored. He asked his father if he might be able to take turns working in the various other stalls and booths. Theseus agreed because he knew this added exposure would be very valuable in the training of Victor. Victor would soon see why some merchants and vendors were more successful than others. He would learn what makes a good salesman, a good merchandiser as well as the value of learning how to deal with people.

"Altogether, Victor was content to stay in the marketplace for only a year and a half. At the age of thirteen and a half, he announced to Theseus that he had learned all he wanted to know about the marketplace. After quizzing him thoroughly, Theseus was inclined to agree, so he asked Victor what he was interested in doing now. He replied that he wanted to do some traveling.

"Although the family enterprises included a number of boats engaged in commerce, as well as caravans, Theseus' family had not done any traveling beyond Poseid. Theseus asked Victor what he had in mind. Victor replied that he would like to go on a caravan journey to the land of the skilled potters. This was a journey to the north and east that took an average of two to three months for a round trip. Theseus did not give him an immediate answer. He would discuss the matter with Hilda.

"Hilda had great confidence in Victor's ability to take care of himself, but like all mothers she was very apprehensive about such a young boy taking such a long journey away from home. Young Iris then went to Hilda and told her of a dream she had had about Victor taking a trip with a caravan. In her dream, the journey was exciting and fruitful and Victor learned many valuable things. Hilda considered the dream prophetic. She knew that Iris was the most gifted seer and communicator in Poseid, even though but a child. She consented to the journey.

"Like any young man about to set out on a great adventurous journey, Victor was filled with excitement and anticipation. He had to wait for five long weeks before the next caravan to the potters' land. They were weeks jammed with preparation. Theseus asked Victor if he would like a traveling companion. He thought it would be a good idea for a trusted friend to accompany Victor. With such an arrangement, they could look out for and perhaps protect one another. Victor liked the idea. Theseus told him that he had in mind to send his trusted friend and assistant, Aeneas. Aeneas could teach him many things along the way which would serve to make the journey even more enjoyable and fruitful. And when they returned, Theseus would consider giving Victor a new job with more responsibility and more pay. Victor beamed at the prospect.

"The day arrived. The caravan departed. Victor was transported not only to the potters' land, but also to a great learning experience. Every day brought its own excitement of discoveries. The changing landscape, the animals seen along the way, the tales of men about their many adventures in past caravans, the different foods, adjusting to constant outdoor living, standing watch at night, observing different customs and cultures along the way, learning not only independence but how to be a valuable part of a team, etc. Aeneas augmented this natural learning process in many ways. He pointed out the value of commerce, for instance. He explained how many people were involved from the time the potter's earth was dug until the finished vessels were finally purchased in the market. His observations and explanations made everything more meaningful.

"More and more, Victor was observing how many skills are required in life just to survive. At one point on their return trip, surviving suddenly became their main concern. They were ruthlessly ambushed by a band of robbers. It was at this moment that Victor fully appreciated the art of self-defense, coupled with preparedness. All experienced caravans are ever alert to the danger of ambush. Not all of them are so capable at defense as was this particular caravan.

"The men of this caravan had been chosen for their ruggedness and fighting spirit. At the first movement of ambush, they had quickly drawn together to form a united team. The attackers suddenly became the defenders as the team of caravan fighters coolly disabled the would-be ambushers one by one, until the lone survivor fled in terror.

"Victor, though frightened, was both exhilarated from the experience and impressed at the power of banding together with control and discipline. Furthermore, he was awed by Aeneas' courage, strength and fighting skill during this threat. On this journey he had grown to greatly admire and respect Aeneas' knowledge, demeanor and self-confidence. Now he realized fully why Theseus had chosen Aeneas to accompany him. What had formerly been great respect widened to include great admiration as well for his companion.

"The remainder of the journey was uneventful. By now Victor was anxious to be home so that he could relate his adventures to his family and friends.

"Theseus was proud of his son. He was also grateful to Aeneas for guiding and protecting Victor so well. He rewarded Aeneas with greater responsibilities and recognition. Aeneas agreed to train Victor as his assistant. Victor was overjoyed.

"Through the next five years the bond of friendship and mutual respect between Victor and Aeneas grew. Minerva and Iris were reaching young womanhood. The family was still close-knit and very loving and caring, each to the other.

"Victor was by now a handsome and powerful young man. His sense of responsibility imbued him with humility. He was soft-spoken, almost shy, but he had a powerful aura of command about him. When he spoke he was listened to with respect. When he asked subordinates or peers to do anything, they did it unquestioningly. He was prepared.

"Suddenly the threat to a peaceful way of life became real. One of the caravans brought news of rumors concerning a planned attack upon Poseid. Some of the ship captains had also heard such rumors. This news reached Theseus, Aeneas and Poseid's governing council at about the same time. Since Theseus was the most respected and powerful man in Poseid, he was asked for advice in coping with the threat. Theseus in turn sought the counsel of Aeneas and Victor.

"Aeneas advised not to act upon rumors. He suggested trying to learn who the potential attackers were, and if possible to learn more of their plans. Victor and Theseus concurred. A plan was outlined and followed to send spies to the conspiring communities to obtain such information. When the spies returned, the information was analyzed. The rumors were verified.

"After consultation with the governing council of Poseid, Aeneas was placed in charge of defending the city and Victor was placed second in command. Aeneas and Victor then called upon those caravan leaders and ship captains known to be friendly and loyal to Poseid for advice and assistance. A system of communication was worked out as well as a plan for defense.

"The enemy had based the success of their attack primarily upon the element of surprise. There was a large element of surprise involved when they finally launched their attack, but it turned out to be the attacker who was surprised and annihilated.

"The success of the defense was due to prescience, preparedness and discipline. The prescience was due to the effective network of communication and to Iris, Victor's sister. The preparedness was due to the hard work and planning of Aeneas and Victor together with their trusted assistants. The discipline was due to Aeneas' and Victor's insistence on a chain of command that followed orders explicitly.

"The communication network had alerted Poseid of the imminence of the attack. A visionary dream by Iris had supplied the details of the manner and exact time of attack.

"Throughout the preparation and the attack, Victor had distinguished himself by his courage, his resourcefulness and his ease of command. It was Victor who led the counterattack against the main enemy force. His every act was a display of valor and coolness. He inspired those under him to many individual acts of heroism.

"News of this cowardly attack upon Poseid spread throughout the known world. News of the total defeat of the attackers alerted any other would-be attackers in the future of the fate they could expect. As a result of Poseid's great victory, it was never again threatened.

"In generations and centuries to follow, Aeneas, Victor, Theseus and Iris all became legends as the story of the great battle was told and re-told.

"Of course, this episode of Hector's incarnation as Victor would not be complete without some reference to Victor's sex life."

"I was beginning to wonder about that, Diane," I interjected.

"Well I hope it's not your prurient interest that makes you wonder, Joseph," she teased.

"A bit of prurience is natural in everyone's life isn't it, Diane," I countered.

"Everyone except the liars, Joseph," she laughed. Then she continued.

"What would you expect of a vigorous, charming and

าan if not an active and expres-
Iilda had raised their children
ibility to them did not mean
. It meant to understand and
ould perhaps term the Posei-
as by no means promiscuous

life which consisted primarily
wo young women from the
e finally paired with one of
ly after the great war. Victor
I and highly compatible. They
happy lives.
into further detail concerning
We have other lifetimes to
discover, so at this point I
"

CHAPTER 6

"Joseph, I think it would be interesting to account to you a few brief episodes from Cassandra's next incarnation, inasmuch as there is a direct connection with Victor and Victoria and with Minerva and Iris.

"From the mental realms, Cassandra saw a marvelous opportunity for growth by incarnating once again in Poseid. By incarnating as the daughter of Victor and Victoria, Hector (Victor) would be her father. Victoria had been the mother of her husband, Ilus, in her first Lemurian lifetime as Naomi. Also, as Naomi, Minerva had been her mother and Iris had been her older sister. From the mental realms, it is always intriguing to take advantage of these interrelationships, whereas from the physical realms it is seldom ever realized!

"So, Cassandra became the first-born of Victor and Victoria. She arrived when Victor was twenty one years of age. She was named Regina. Her arrival in Poseid as Regina took place twenty two years after her departure as Cyntha. This was a most interesting occurrence considering Cyntha's role in the recent development of Poseid.

"From the moment of her birth, Regina was greatly loved. It would be difficult to describe the outpouring and intensity of love that came from Minerva and Iris, her two special aunts who had been mother and sister respectively in the past. As for Victor, his bond with Regina was the closest and strongest of all. Victoria loved her as only a mother can love a first-born, a love that was further strengthened by the unseen bond of their past relationship. It was indeed fitting that Regina should grow up in such a strong environment of love, which she herself had helped shape and inculcate through her immediate past life in the Earth.

"As her mother in Lemuria, it was Minerva who had first influenced Naomi's interest in weaving. It was Minerva who had inspired Cyntha from the mental realms to re-invent the loom. It was Minerva who would teach Regina many valuable lessons of womanhood.

"Iris was respected as the greatest oracle in Poseid, many thought in the whole world. At an early age, Regina expressed strong interest in this ability and never missed an opportunity to be with Iris, or to question her about these mysteries. It was Iris, for example, who explained to her the puzzle of deja vu. Deja vu, of course, is the experience of going somewhere you have never been, and recognizing your surroundings as being familiar. The same applies to persons or events. Everyone has this experience once or frequently in their lifetime, and many explanations have been suggested for its cause. Here is the explanation given to Regina by Iris."

"The reason that so many places in Poseid seem familiar to you, Regina, is because they are," explained Iris. "You do not remember it, but quite recently you had a long lifetime here. That is why, in this lifetime, you cannot go anywhere without having that peculiar feeling that you have been there before. That is also why there is such a strong attachment and deep love between us, you and me, because we have spent past lives together. That is the reason for the great love that flows between you and your father, your mother and your Aunt Minerva. We are all very closely connected in many ways.

"Another reason that so many places you have never been seem familiar when you first see them is because you have been there while you were sleeping. Our spirit forms leave our bodies when we sleep and travel to many places and realms. Sometimes we remember when we awaken. Most of the time we do not, unless we visit that same place while awake. There is a logical explanation for everything in our lives, once we learn to use our various abilities to find the answer," Iris concluded.

"From that lifetime on, Cassandra had a deep attraction and interest in all matters dealing with the mystical, the psychic and the supernatural," Michael continued. "You remember how strong her desire was for the gift of prophecy in her lifetime as Cassandra.

"Thirty nine thousand years was to pass before Atlantis reached its potential as a civilization. For thousands of years, Poseid remained the major city in the Earth, though it was by no means major in relation to what it was to become. Its population fluctuated between 100,000 and 300,000 during those years. Meanwhile several other major cities were born in Atlantis and in several other parts of the Earth.

"During that span of time, Cassandra elected to incarnate frequently. She experienced life as a black woman, a yellow woman, a red woman and a brown woman. She would have been white too except for the fact that the white race was not yet upon the Earth. Sometimes she would resort to her old skills of weaving and creating garments. Other times she would develop new skills such as a female witch doctor, a teacher, various kinds of artisans, a prostitute, a religious person, a ruler, a peasant. In all, she incarnated a total of sixty more times during that thirty nine thousand year span, for an overall total of seventy five incarnations.

"Quite obviously, she was amassing a large number of skills, all of which were being duly recorded in her subconscious mind. It is a matter of absolute fact that the subconscious mind does indeed function like the memory bank of a giant computer, recording and retaining all data perceived through all the senses. It is also a fact that the subconscious mind can feed this data back to the conscious mind as either retrieved data or as learned response. In Cassandra's case, the most persistent data being stored in her memory was data of womanhood in all of its various aspects that she was experiencing. The subconscious mind does not have the power of discrimination. That is the function of the conscious mind. The subconscious is like a sponge. It simply absorbs whatever is contacted through the senses. So, in addition to all of those skills that Cassandra was acquiring, her subconscious mind was also absorbing a very large number of habit patterns, or engrams—both good and bad, both beneficial and harmful, both progressive and regressive.

"Unfortunately, the harmful patterns that are imprinted upon the subconscious mind of a person who is physically incarnated, can only be dealt with from the physical level. When you leave the physical body and return to the mental or the spiritual realms, you can not wave your magic wand and change all those negative patterns acquired in the physical body. The only way that such negative or harmful patterns can be changed is in a subsequent physical incarnation. That is the main reason why the physical worlds are the most difficult of all realms to master. Those who do master the physical are masters of all other realms as well.

"Therefore, Joseph, if people will take this information that I am now giving you, and apply it in their lives, there is the possibility that they can attain self-mastery in this one life. Let me illustrate just a little bit more the subjective power and force with which the subconscious mind can hold one in virtual slavery.

"I ask you to think of as many habits as possible that you have acquired in this lifetime. Think of 'good' habits as well as 'bad' ones. Think of the habits of eating and taste that enslave you to improper nutritional habits even when you know better and want to change. Think of personality habits in your interrelationships that you know are objectionable, but which you still haven't changed because they are so ingrained, so 'automatic.' Think of the habit pattern of avoiding those things which you know are necessary to your best interest such as regular exercise. Think of the tendencies you may have to engage in negative thought patterns. There is practically no limit to our habit patterns. The point that I wish to make, however, is to illustrate to you how difficult it is to change just one habit. It requires a constant act of will, and it further requires that the old habit be replaced by another habit, hopefully a desired one. You cannot simply conquer an old habit and leave a vacuum. You must replace it.

"Now, the reason some of our habits are so deeply ingrained is because they have been established and refortified over many lifetimes, many incarnations. Is it any wonder that the habit pattern is so compelling in such a case? If we can acquire a habit in a matter of weeks or months that is difficult to break, how much more so the difficulty in changing a habit pattern of many lifetimes!

"These habit patterns apply to every single area of one's life. Over a series of lifetimes, some of the most harmful habits are those dealing with our value systems such as religions, political philosophies, moral judgments, etc. These value system habit patterns are invariably highly charged with emotion. The greater the emotion, the more indelible the engram that is imprinted upon the subconscious memory pattern, and consequently the more difficult to change. In most instances where the subconscious is deeply impressed with such emotional convictions, there is not sufficient open-mindedness to institute a change.

"Still, this is no reason for one to be discouraged. If one understands the actual mechanics, the scientific cause and effect, of habit formation and restructuring, then such a one can begin to reshape their lives into whatever patterns they truly desire.

"Having skimmed lightly over sixty of Cassandra's lifetimes, we come now to a major incarnation in the great continent of Atlantis in the world's greatest city, Poseid. The flourishing family business which Cyntha had helped to create had long since disappeared. After thirty nine thousand years, nothing remained the same except the geographical location of Poseid. Even so, the topography was substantially different. What had been a coastal city about twelve feet above sea level was now a coastal city of perhaps fifty feet elevation. The legends which were born during the lifetime of Cyntha had grown to become the mythology of Ancient Atlantis. Although the facts were substantially accurate, the principle characters had become gods and goddesses in the constant retelling. And the ironic fact was that many of those same 'gods and goddesses' were now reincarnating in the city which gave birth to the legends, and they had no recall of the actual events at all.

"To gain a perspective of Atlantis at that time, we have but to look at the United States today. Atlantis led the Earth in power and in technology. In some important ways, the technology of Atlantis was more advanced. A major difference was in the population of Atlantis and of the Earth as a whole. At that time the Earth's population fluctuated between 200,000,000 and 275,000,000. There were not nearly as many populous cities. The urban areas of the Earth were concentrated in a relatively few cities and accounted for perhaps 50,000,000 people. The rest of the population covered the spectrum from rural, pastoral and rustic, to primitive, barbaric and savage.

"In this connection, it helps to think of the Earth in terms of a classroom. At any given time, the population will reflect both the quantity and the quality of the cosmic education process.

"In the entire continent of Atlantis, the population numbered about 55,000,000. Poseid numbered about 1,700,000. Concentrated in that 1,700,000 were many of the Earth's greatest thinkers, scientists, technicians, philosophers, teachers, inventors, craftsmen, artisans, humanists, deists, religionists, doctors, lawmakers, musicians, artists, writers and builders. After thousands and thousands of years, a great civilization had once again risen to provide the people of Earth with an opportunity to truly advance their consciousness to a higher level.

"The merger of so many of the Earth's advanced humans in Poseid had produced marvels of technology, the sciences and arts, spiritual enlightenment and progress in general. There was abundant electrical energy, produced through utilization of Earth's natural grids and currents. This energy was transmitted without the use of wires. Ecology was the way of life. Pollution was practically non-existent. There was public transportation by means of electrical cars which moved constantly on the city streets and were free. There was a system of exchange that did not involve money, but instead placed a value upon one's services to society as measured in energy units, thus eliminating severe economic cycles. The healing arts were far more advanced than in the Earth today. In Poseid, all of the many disciplines and approaches to healing were respected and utilized. The ruling council was structured in such a manner that the leadership was automatically vested in the most able without the necessity or gamble of elections. Agriculturally, there was great variety and plentiful supply. There were formal educational requirements that were enlightened compared to your standards of today.

"Lest I give you the false impression that this was a perfect society, let me hasten to say that the seeds for the downfall of this great civilization were even then being sown. But more on that later.

"One very important aspect of the Poseidan culture that is still lacking in the Earth today, was the open communication and visitations that existed with space brothers from some of the other planets and physical worlds beyond the Earth. Many of your present day scientists would laugh and scoff at such conjecture, yet the fact remains that it was so. The evidence of some of those ancient encounters still exists to this day in many places on the Earth.

CHAPTER 7

"Cassandra's incarnation into this culture would produce experiences vastly different from any of her previous
lifetimes. Accordingly, she spent much time preparing herself in the mental realms.

"Finally, her preparations were complete. She had selected as her father the most renowned horticulturist in
the Earth at that time. His name was Aristaeus. Aristaeus
was a great and noble soul of many incarnations in the
physical body. It was rumored by some that he had been
fathered by a prince of godly lineage from the constellation
Musca. Such a rumor would not be considered unusual
for it was a frequent occurrence for visitors from other
worlds to journey to the Earth and Poseid was their main
destination. It was also customary in that culture for
such visitors to be offered sexual companionship during
their sojourn, and offspring frequently came from such
unions.

"Aristaeus' wife, Latona, was of true aristocratic birth.
Her father Coeus had been the previous ruler of Poseid
until his death. Her mother Phoebe likewise shared the
lineage of the enlightened ruling aristocracy. Phoebe had
imparted to her daughter, Latona, all of those qualities
of bearing and breeding that one associates as applicable

to the idealized woman. Cassandra felt assured that Latona would in turn impart those attributes to her.

"Cassandra chose to be the firstborn of Aristaeus and Latona, and she also chose to be called Cassandra, which she was. Five years later Latona bore twins, a boy and a girl. The boy was named Apollo and the girl, Artemis.

"For the first five years of that life, Cassandra received the undivided attention of Latona's gentle love and guidance in the ways of being female. So, by age five, Cassandra was already a highly poised and delightful little girl to behold. The attention given to this precious child was likewise shared by Aristaeus in many ways. He delighted in showing Cassandra his beautiful farms, gardens and orchards. He explained to her the marvels of growing things in cooperation with the various other nature kingdoms such as bees and the little unseen elemental beings to whom Aristaeus frequently talked. Obviously Aristaeus knew what he was talking about, since he was widely acknowledged to be the foremost horticulturist in the world.

"Cassandra was particularly fascinated by the bees, and she would observe their activities for hours in the farms, gardens and orchards. Aristaeus was the world's leading producer of honey, as well as the leading authority on bees, and he never tired of explaining their mysteries to Cassandra. It was frequently said that Aristaeus' honey was the best in the world because his bees were the happiest.

"It was a delighted family that welcomed twins into their world when Cassandra was five. In many respects, you would have thought they were Cassandra's. She was now old enough to enjoy and appreciate them without being jealous of any attention taken away from her. She was mother's special little helper. As the twins grew, they were molded in much the same manner as Cassandra, except of course that Apollo was a very masculine little boy. The devotion amongst and between the three children was remarkable and touching.

"Growing up together was an extraordinary experience of fun and joy. You must appreciate that all three children were very highly evolved souls. They had incarnated together into an environment which would allow them to appreciate and enjoy the best of what the physical world had to offer at that time. They had enlightened parents and influential friends. They were in the greatest city in the world and they had the means to take advantage of whatever cultural opportunities pleased them. They were intelligent, they were beautiful, they were wealthy, yet they were not spoiled. They had been raised to be responsible and productive. They therefore had countless options available to them as to how they would spend their lives. For Cassandra, that time was now approaching for such a decision to be made.

"Having experienced so much of what life had to offer in a Utopian environment, Cassandra decided that she should devote herself to those things which brought her the most pleasure and sense of fulfillment. She was by now accomplished in the arts, both from the point of view of appreciation and taste as well as from the skills of creativity and execution. She therefore decided to focus her primary vocational efforts on music, painting, sculpture and the cultivation of psychic skills.

"Cassandra had a beautiful voice which she very ably accompanied on a lyre-like instrument quite popular at the time. Most of her songs were original compositions which seemed to flow from her lips spontaneously as if inspired from another world. Whenever she picked up her lyre to play and sing, life around her came to a standstill as everyone instantly fell under the mesmerizing influence of her angelic songs.

"Aristaeus' home was filled with Cassandra's paintings. Her style was delicate, yet paradoxically very forceful. Most of her work was in pastels. She preferred to sit before a canvas without any preconceived ideas and let her painting flow as effortlessly as the songs from her lips. She often had no idea what she was going to paint until the painting was at least partially completed. Nevertheless, most of her paintings contained people enveloped in ethereal surroundings. Cassandra's works were so admired by the many frequent visitors and guests, that they would often prevail upon Cassandra to paint for them. As a result, many of Cassandra's treasures hung in the homes of many of Poseid's most influential citizens.

"Not only paintings, but sculptures also adorned Aristaeus' home. These sculptures were predominantly the work of Cassandra. They consisted mostly of busts at this point, but she was now beginning to experiment successfully with full forms and with animals, birds and various objects.

"Friends were often astounded at the range of Cassandra's artistic talents, and would frequently ask her how she acquired such a broad range of creative ability. When pinned down, Cassandra would usually attribute much of her originality and inventiveness to her psychic perceptivity. The true answer, of course, was that the learned skills of many lifetimes were flowing freely from her subconscious mind. Cassandra's intense interest in psychic matters merely facilitated this flow. In the final analysis, Cassandra's psychic interests and sensitivity would lead her to deep spiritual growth and understanding in this lifetime.

"Among the many friends and acquaintances that visited Aristaeus' home, there were inevitably those select few who were greatly attracted to the psychic level of life. At first, this led merely to parlor type games of mind reading and attempts at communicating with discarnate beings. Eventually, it led to a grouping of six individuals who were sincerely seeking the answers to many of life's deeper mysteries and hidden meanings. The six consisted of Cassandra, Apollo, Artemis, Victor, Iris and Aeneas. You may recall, Iris had been the youngest sister of Victor in the earliest days of Atlantis. She had also been the older sister of Naomi in Lemuria. She was the great psychic, mystic and prophetess who helped save Poseid in its infancy. Victor and Naomi were Hector and Cassandra in previous lives. In this particular life, Iris was to be the wife of Aeneas. This was the Aeneas from Iris' former life as Iris. In that former life, Aeneas had been the assistant of Theseus, and he had been a great leader in his own right. Victor was again the name chosen by Hector for this life.

"While Aeneas was not always physically included in this close knit group of six, he was very much a part of their undertaking in principle and in spirit, if you'll forgive the pun. He would doubtless have been a more active member of the group had his great responsibilities and busy schedule permitted regular participation. In this life, Aeneas was the greatest engineer-builder in Poseid and was also a member of the ruling council of Atlantis.

CHAPTER 8

"Atlantis was such an extraordinary civilization at that time that I would like to give you at least a brief insight into its technology and culture. Probably no other city of its size that ever existed in the Earth could boast of the diversity of accomplishment or life style of Poseid. It often seemed that each of its million plus inhabitants must have possessed many talents to have created so many wonders with so few hands. However, when you recall that this great city was many thousands of years in developing, then you will realize that the many marvels of Poseid did not appear in one lifetime. Also, there was the fact that Poseid had never been destroyed by war or natural disaster. Therefore, many buildings and technologies were quite ancient.

"We have mentioned earlier in our story that Atlantis was not heavily populated by present day population standards. The entire continent was about 55,000,000, which was perhaps a little more than one-fourth of the total Earth population. There was a marvelous diversity of life styles for an incoming soul to choose from, ranging from the most primitive to the most civilized. Poseid was the major city of all Atlantis and of the Earth. There were eleven lesser cities of Atlantis that varied in size from

20,000 to 750,000. The city next largest in size to Poseid was located East of the present great city of New York and now lies submerged beneath the ocean.

"Most of the very great souls of Atlantis are presently incarnated in the earth, and a majority of them are in the United States. There is a very definite purpose and reason for this which we will state later. The reason that the earth is more heavily populated now than it has ever been is obvious. This is the end of time. For that reason, those souls who have been participating in the unfoldment of the Divine Plan for eons want to be in on the final drama.

"It is true that many former Atlanteans who are now in the Earth remember bits and pieces of one or more of their past lives. It is likely therefore that some will recall parts of what I am now mentioning. If there seem to be conflicts between their memory and what is related here, simply remind them that there was a span of well over a thousand years when Poseid was at its peak. Where there seems to be disagreement may be because their incarnation was either not in Poseid or else it was in a time sequence before or after events stated here. In any event, there is nothing for you to defend.

"The term 'wholistic or holistic healing' has recently come into vogue in the earth to describe a more total approach to the healing process. It means a cooperative blending of the healing disciplines and arts in the diagnosis and treatment of illnesses. It may interest you to know that Poseid had the most complete and advanced center of this type the earth has ever known. Many of those souls who created this center are now in the earth working toward the reestablishment of this concept. It was a far cry from the predominantly allopathic procedures still practiced in the earth by the majority of physicians. It is not our purpose to lecture earth in the practices of healing, but only to point out that you still have a way to go to reach the level attained in ancient Atlantis.

"I mentioned to you that Aristaeus was the foremost horticulturist in the earth at that time. Horticulture, too, was quite advanced in Atlantis under the overall influence of Aristaeus, who was the Minister of Agriculture in the ruling council. As with health, more basic and natural methods were used in agriculture in Atlantis than are now used or understood in the earth. Due to their understanding of the natural forces and controls in nature, they did not find it necessary to use pesticides or herbicides to protect growing crops. Nor did they have the necessity to use harsh synthetic chemical fertilizers. They used friendly insects and birds to keep out unfriendly pests. They worked closely with the processes of the Earth as a living being. Accordingly, they were able to energize water and other plant nutrients which produced crops of enormous yields and vitality.

"No mention of the culture of Atlantis would be complete without reference to the educational options and practices. There were three basic approaches or options available to parents. There was the day school, the boarding school and the home school. The day school was similar to your present typical public and private day schools. It was considerably more individualized and effective however. There was not your stereotyped curriculum. The process was geared to discovering, utilizing and developing the natural talents and abilities of each child. The same learning tools were available to all children, regardless of which option the parents chose. These tools consisted of access to a central computer, various kinds of learning machines including television and a balanced approach to education. Along with the basics necessary to language and communication skills, children were taught a balanced approach to sexuality, general health and nutrition, exercise and total body care and how to utilize the creativeness inherent in all of us. Education and learning was made fun, exciting and rewarding. The fun and excitement are natural to a wholesome learning and teaching process. The rewards built in to the Atlantean method were actual monetary type compensation available to everyone for each contribution to the body of knowledge. For example, all known information and knowledge was recorded on the central computer memory file. Anyone adding to this fund of knowledge was rewarded financially commensurate with the value of the knowledge contributed. A most compelling incentive.

"The boarding schools were for orphans, for parents who did not want children and for children who did not want parents. Needless to say, those who supervised these schools were especially qualified to deal with the inherent psychological and soul problems involved. We think it was a far more enlightened way to deal with those situations than now exists in the earth.

"The home school was simply the parents accepting responsibility for the education of their children in their own home. The technology consisted of direct linkup with the home television and the central computer. The television provided instrumentation for direct inquiry with the computer. Accordingly, any question which you could formulate was answerable if the information existed. Apart from this, the finest teachers in the world on every subject were available on command from the home television receiver. The economics of this technology were actually much cheaper than supporting your present-day type of public schools with so many teachers, so many buildings and real estate and so much mediocrity, nonsense and politics. While not perfect, the system was far more enlightened and effective than now exists in the earth.

"The economics and medium of exchange of Atlantis has no counterpart in your world today, insofar as a system that is actually functioning. A similar type system has been developed, but it is not in operation. Therefore it is only hypothetical and theoretical. The vested interests in the earth are not going to allow such an arrangement as long as they are in control. The Atlantean economic system did not utilize currency. People were not paid in money for their goods and services. Money and currency systems allow for unlimited manipulation and abuse by governments and wealthy individuals.

"What was used in Atlantis was a method whereby values were placed upon every conceivable type of job, occupation and profession. This system was refined over a period of several hundred years. In practice, energy units were earned according to the complexity and value to society of every form of work contribution. These energy units could be saved just like money or they could be 'spent' for goods and services just like money. These energy units could also be loaned or borrowed like money. However, one could not be robbed of their savings by inflation or economic manipulation or at the point of a weapon. If you became dissatisfied with your economic status in life, you could always reeducate yourself to a higher value to society. Both you and society would benefit from your added skills and value.

"Electrical power generation was of several types. The energy for the masses of urban dwellers was mostly produced at central energy-gathering focus points on a gigantic grid. The earth is completely laced with rivers of energy which circulate below the ground and above the ground. At certain points on the earth, the underground rivers of current intersect with the atmospheric rivers of current. Where these intersections take place, it is possible to construct a tower type of building so that an actual connection can be made between the two types of energy currents. Within such a structure, the energy currents can be tapped and channeled to a central crystal device which then blends the two polarities into a usable direct current which can then be transmitted from the same tower to any place on the grid without the need for wires. The grid itself is not man-made, but is part of the invisible lines of force which reticulate the planet. Anyone located on or very close to the grid lines could then be supplied with power.

"For those not able to benefit from the above type of power generation, there were other devices which could be used. One was a portable generating device approximately two cubic feet in size. This device consisted of a series of spheres on spokes around an axle. The spheres were compartmented in such a way that mercury partially filled one of the compartments in each sphere. The other compartments contained special gases. At the opposite end of the axle shaft was an armature device which generated electrical energy when the shaft rotated. Once the shaft was placed in rotation by a charge of static electricity, the rotation became perpetual because of the unique properties of mercury and the unique placement of the mercury in the spheres and the unique placement of the spheres on the spokes from the axle.

"Other than these two examples, there was also hydroelectric power and windmill electric power. Specially constructed crystals were used as storage batteries. Such crystals could store unbelievably immense charges of electrical energy. So as you can see, your scientists have a lot to learn about 'clean' energy production.

"Most of the residents of Poseid lived in apartment structures. These apartments were of great variety in architectural expression of design, construction and esthetics. They ranged in age from new to hundreds of years old. However, even most of the old ones were very attractive and sound. The basic building material was a form of concrete type substance which was very strong, waterproof, durable and quite attractive.

"The majority of the housing was owned by the government and was rented for very nominal amounts. Unlike the public housing that you are accustomed to today, the Atlantean housing was maintained with considerable pride by both the government and the residents.

"Private ownership was allowed, but most people preferred the convenience and low cost of government-owned housing. Because of the durability of the homes, most of them had long since paid for themselves. Therefore, a major portion of the rent monies were used for constant maintenance and modernization. The homes boasted of such conveniences as your most modern homes of today. For example, the lighting consisted of panels inserted in the walls and ceilings which could be made to glow in various colors and intensity. There were also machines to do your laundry, cooking, refrigeration, etc. Needless to say, all apartments had plumbing which would be considered modern by your standards.

"The overall beauty of Poseid has no equal in the earth today. The people took great pride in cultivating their surroundings with the most breathtakingly beautiful arrangements of architectural landscaping and ornamental combinations. There were many employees of the government who were highly skilled and dedicated to creating, maintaining and preserving the visual wonders of nature. Aristaeus was both their leader and their inspiration. It was under his guidance that Poseid had reached this pinnacle of visual expression. It was under his guidance, too, that his beautiful daughter, Cassandra, could taste and appreciate the loveliness of life in a physical body as it was meant to be lived.

"With the constant inspiration of such beautiful and harmonious surroundings, it was only natural that the arts should flourish in Poseid. Everywhere, there was evidence of man trying to compete with nature to produce even greater beauty. Statues abounded. Architectural embellishments accentuated the horticultural achievements. Paintings and crafts were evidenced in every home and office. Music and dance were appreciated and participated in by all. Speaking of music, almost everyone played a musical instrument. Music has a very great affect upon the lives of human beings. I think that probably in Atlantis, most people realized this and used music in the most constructive of ways to balance and bring joy to their lives. Dancing, too, was recognized as a most enjoyable and therapeutic pursuit. Consequently, the life of the average Atlantean in Poseid was abundantly rich in artistic appreciation and participation.

"While television provided the predominant entertainment for the average Atlantean, there was also live theater. Poseid had two magnificent outdoor theaters. One was in the round, so to speak, in which the actors performed on a stage in the center of the audience. The other was a conventional open air style in which the actors performed in front of their audience. There was also a huge center for indoor theater and sports.

"There were no professional sports teams at this time, but there were a number of amateur teams competing in many kinds of games and contests. Wagering existed, but it was not of an organized nature.

"In many ways, everyday life in Poseid was remarkably close to everyday life in parts of the earth today, but without nearly so many stresses and major problems, and for the most part with a far greater appreciation of life.

"Manufacturing facilities were scattered amongst the twelve cities mentioned, different ones specializing in products that required the skills predominant to the area. There was no network of roads and highways such as exists in the United States today. There were major road-ways connecting the cities, however, and intelligently planned streets within the cities. Local public transporta-tion was free and was provided by electric vehicles which moved continuously and frequently throughout the urban areas. People walked a lot and used bicycles for most of their daily commuting. In traveling to more distant places, people used boats or aircraft most of the time. Boats were powered by sail and by electric motors driven by crystal batteries and larger versions of the mercury-sphere-armature device described before. The aircraft uti-lized a technology that neutralized gravity while providing a propulsion of up to one thousand miles an hour. All manufactured products were constructed of the finest and most durable of materials to insure the longest possible useful life. The highest level of skill went into their fabrica-tion. Planned obsolescence was not considered good for the economy, but an unnecessary waste of human and natural resources.

"There were a number of ways that one could become wealthy, even though the economy was controlled by the governing council. Since money and its selfish use could not debase or neutralize genuine contributions to society, it was a simple matter to reward work, inventiveness, creativity, new knowledge, etc. on a basis of the actual benefit to society. For example, if someone invented a new device that would enhance life, that device would be manufactured by an existing or a new government controlled company. The inventor would receive a royalty for each item sold for as long as he lived. The royalty would cease on the death of the inventor. New contributions to knowledge were accorded a value as objectively as possible and a suitable royalty was likewise paid to the contributor for life. One could become wealthy by horticulture, such as Aristaeus, by writing, by composing, by performing, etc. Becoming wealthy wasn't the goal of most citizens because wealth wasn't necessary to live a rich and fulfilling life.

"The culture of Atlantis, and particularly Poseid, provided the opportunity for meeting fellow human beings from other planets on their frequent visits to the earth. It also provided on occasion for a lucky few to visit other planets. In those days there was open communication and scientific and cultural exchange with our brothers from other worlds.

"The ruling council of Atlantis consisted of twelve members, one person from each of the twelve largest cities. Such esteem and value was placed upon the attainment of consciousness and awareness, that it was through such attainment that the twelve representatives were selected by their respective communities. Each of the twelve cities was also governed by a council of twelve, one of whom was selected by his peers to serve on the supreme council. The twelve member council of each city and the twelve member supreme council of Atlantis each selected one of their number to act as chairman of the respective councils. So much respect was accorded to the chairman that he or she was given the power of veto which then required nine votes to overrule. Such a system of government could best be described as spiritual rather than political. It was not spiritual in the religious sense. It was spiritual in the sense that the highest value was placed upon the development and functional use of those godlike spiritual faculties that are inherent, but mostly dormant, in all human beings.

"Before returning to the principle characters of our story, I would like to mention one more thing with regards to the culture of Atlantis. Communications. At the heart of every great human being, every God, every civilization, is a large degree of mastery of the art and science of communication. Those of lesser consciousness take communication for granted. The hallmark of an expanded consciousness is the realization that nothing in all the universe is more important than communication. Communication implies both a transmission and a reception of a thought, an idea, an impression, a feeling, a mood, an emotion. To be complete, communication must result in a knowing, an understanding and a comprehension of that which has been received. For example, in order for us to communicate this story to you, you must be capable of receiving it telepathically. You must also understand, comprehend and apprehend the meaning, the essence and the implications of what is being expressed to you. You must have a practical vocabulary sufficient to synthesize the words into the same foundation of ideas that we intend to communicate to you.

"Having communicated our concept of communication, I would now like to state that the technology of Atlantis and the consciousness of its leaders produced the highest and greatest level of communication that man in the earth has experienced in millions of years. A good level of communication existed amongst the leaders and between the leaders and the citizens. In a number of instances, there was good communication between man and the animals as well as between man and the elements and man and the other nature kingdoms. Generally speaking, there was a much wider communication between man in the flesh and those of us in the mental and spiritual realms. And there was also frequent communication between Atlanteans and those from other physical worlds.

"Perhaps the most important of all forms of communication is that which enables a human being to make viable contact with one's own self. By that, I mean the capacity to reach within one's own consciousness to discover and communicate with one's very own soul. To gain this ability is to strip away all of the layers and coatings of countless lifetimes, and stand bare and naked before the pure, essential essence of love. To gain this ability is to gain the understanding of all men, of all life, of yourself. To gain this ability is the end and purpose of living. To reach this goal puts us in touch with our own God nature.

"You must forgive me if I get carried away from time to time in my own efforts at communication. The last thing that Diane and I want to communicate in this story is that we are preaching. I know that you understand that it is only our genuine love for mankind that tempts us to reveal so much. We feel so strongly that if man in the Earth truly understood the realities and options of eternal living, surely man would make the right choices for saving himself and the planet.

"Diane is suggesting to me, Joseph, that now would be a good time to fill you in on Hector's life as Victor. So without further comment, I'll move aside and continue later," Michael concluded.

CHAPTER 9

"This is the best time to fill you in on Hector's life as Victor during this particular incarnation," Diane commenced. "It is already obvious that there was a close association with Cassandra.

"Hector, like Cassandra, planned this important incarnation very carefully. This was to be the fulfillment of all previous Earth lives as well as the firm foundation for the remaining physical lives to come. Accordingly, it was Hector's plan (as well as the Divine Plan) to select those parents that would provide the basis for the most opportunities.

"Cronus was the chairman of the governing council of Poseid. He was fifty eight years old and enormously respected by his countrymen. Over his lifetime he had contributed greatly to the fund of knowledge in the earth. His contributions ranged from healing procedures to archaeology, to writing, to inventing advanced technological concepts. More important, he was a man of vast spiritual depth and understanding. Cronus was such an advanced soul that he had developed his powers of communication to the point of cosmic consciousness. He frequently communicated by telepathy with beings beyond the physical worlds. It was through such communication that he agreed to be Hector's father.

"After the initial contact with Hector through telepathy, Cronus discussed the matter thoroughly with his lovely wife, Rhea. Cronus had married Rhea when he was forty five years of age and Rhea was twenty two. Rhea was now thirty five. Although they hadn't planned to have any children, the idea was appealing to them. When Cronus told Rhea that Hector had been their child, Ilus, many thousands of years ago in the ancient city of Xanthia in the land of Lemuria, Rhea became ecstatic with the idea. Cronus then told Rhea the story of their lifetime together when he was Aladran of Xanthia, and of their sons Ilus and Virga. He also related to her how she had been Cassandra's mother (Rhea) during the earliest days of Atlantis, and how she had been married during that lifetime to Byrten, her former son, Virga. Rhea, though not as advanced as Cronus, was nevertheless a very advanced soul. She was intrigued by this revelation as well as by the fact that ancient friends often remain together in one relationship or another through the ages. It is most often this type of soul connection that creates instant bonds of love or hate when we meet someone with whom we have shared a past life.

"Hector discussed with Cronus the major goals he had in mind for his life as Victor. Cronus agreed to provide the environment and guidance to achieve those goals.

"It was an easy pregnancy. During the course of the fetal development, Rhea learned to communicate with Hector. Hector for his part guided Rhea very carefully in matters of diet, rest, exercise and psychological preparation. By the marvelous 'coincidence' of good planning, Rhea's best friend Latona was also pregnant with Cassandra. Latona and her husband, Aristaeus, had undergone a similar experience in agreeing to be Cassandra's parents.

"Victor was born. After seventy five prior incarnations in the earth, this was to be the culmination, promise and fulfillment of all those lifetimes.

"As a little boy, Victor was very curious and mischievous. He never seemed to run out of energy. But what healthy little boy does for that matter? Like many small children, Victor had an invisible playmate. Unlike the parents of many small children, Victor's parents did not interfere with this relationship. Cronus, in his wisdom, knew that this invisible friend of Victor's was Virga. Virga, as you now recall, was Ilus' brother when they were sons of Aladran (Cronus). The approval of this relationship provided the foundation for a profound early development of the psychic capacities of Victor. Virga would remain his companion for many years.

"By agreement, Cronus and Rhea directed Victor's early attention to the arts as well as scientific studies and sports. By the time Victor was seven he was goal oriented, precocious and disciplined. This is not to imply that he did not enjoy the freedoms and unstructured pastimes of small boys. Quite the contrary was true. Cronus and Rhea carefully guided him to a balanced appreciation and use of time. Victor was a happy child. He was filled with goodness and love. If anything, he trusted others too much. Even in these most utopian of Atlantean days, it could be very costly to trust so blindly. Cronus and Rhea would have to temper that trust with some caution and discernment.

"Victor did not attend a public school. He was one of many children whose parents chose the option of home school as previously described by Michael. He did have a tutor for a few years to provide the proper direction and discipline in the arts and sciences. By the time he was nine this was no longer necessary.

"Among Cronus' and Rhea's circle of friends, there was the custom of parents bringing their children together frequently for games, recreation and group interaction. This provided the necessary balance that the children would have missed by not attending public schools. It was in this setting that Victor and Cassandra first met and were drawn to each other. They were so much alike in their tastes, abilities and interests. From the first, they became sweethearts and were virtually inseparable during those group encounters. Also, from time to time the families of Aristaeus and Cronus would visit one another. Victor and Cassandra enjoyed these visits the most because it allowed them to be with each other without the group distraction.

"The relationship of Victor and Cassandra continued in this manner until they were thirteen. By that time they were both emotionally mature beyond their years. Physically, too, they had developed beyond the average. Sexually, they had both been active for about two years. Until this time, however, their sexual experience had been only with their own body. Neither had experienced sexual intercourse with another. On one of those family visits to Aristaeus' home, this changed. One beautiful spring day Cassandra and Victor went for a walk in the fields beyond the groves and pastures that surrounded Aristaeus' home. They were so swept up in the enchantment of the beauty that surrounded them, and in the love that drew them together, that they lay down in the field and embraced one another. Having tasted the thrill of embrace, they could no longer resist the urge for mutual exploration that led quickly and inevitably to their physical union. This was an experience far beyond anything that had happened to either of them before. They were absolutely intoxicated with one another.

"For the remainder of that spring they could focus their minds or attention on little else than their maneuvers to be together. They were together often. Others were aware of the liaison, but knew that it was to be allowed through the end of spring. Virga, for one, was communicating to Victor that this relationship would not be allowed to be permanent. Both sets of parents discussed the matter openly amongst themselves and agreed that the relationship was preordained but that it was permissible to continue only until summer. Virga and the parents all knew that the life plans for Cassandra and Victor called for them to be married to someone else.

"With the approach of summer, Cronus finalized plans for the most exciting adventure of Victor's life. This adventure was designed to distract Victor from his total preoccupation with thoughts of Cassandra, as well as to provide him with an incredible background for his coming leadership role in Atlantis. Unbeknown to Victor, he was soon to experience a thrill available to only a few in the earth. He was going on a space journey. While this journey would not make him forget about Cassandra, it would fill his mind with so many phenomena that it would make the parting less painful.

"At that time, earth was visited by space brothers from both within and beyond our solar system. The most intelligent, the most technologically advanced and the most powerful of those beings were from the three planet system of Arcturus. They were known (and still are) as the Novic people. Their leader was known as Prime Nova.

Although they resembled earth beings in many ways, they were quite different in many ways. Their average height was between three and four feet. Their bodies were not fleshy like yours, but were rocklike. Their atomic structure was silicon based rather than carbon based. They were extremely powerful physically. In spite of their small stature, they were far stronger than any earth man. You may find it strange to believe, but they did not die. They could be destroyed, but they could not die. Their great age accounted for their extreme intelligence. Also, they did not feel things emotionally like we do. They found the emotional nature of flesh and blood humans difficult to understand and relate to. The Novic people ruled literally millions upon millions of worlds. They were a benevolent people who had long since learned of the futility of war. Nevertheless, they were the most powerful militarily of all space people. Prime Nova stated on more than one occasion that their computer systems were the most extensive and sophisticated in all the universe. Technologically, they could transcend time and therefore they were not bound by the limitations of the finite, physical worlds. They could travel backward or forward in time. For countless thousands of years they had observed all of the physical worlds in this entire sector of space. Through their communication with the spirit and mental realms and their observation of the physical worlds during that great span of time, they had discovered that the planet Earth was indeed the center and focal point for the unfolding of the Divine Plan. Furthermore, they were in charge of protecting as many of the physical worlds as possible from the negative factor forces. Their special attention was directed to the protection of the earth awaiting the advent of the Baby God.

"Victor could not believe his good fortune when Cronus told him of his coming space journey. He was so excited thinking of all of the ramifications of such a trip that he momentarily forgot that this would take him away from his beloved Cassandra. When he did recover his presence of mind in this respect, he asked Cronus if there was any possibility that Cassandra might also share this experience. Cronus patiently explained to him that this was not possible. Victor was then gripped with an ambivalence that seldom could be matched in the affairs of life. He was torn between the pain of leaving his great love and the unparalleled opportunity of the greatest of adventures. The fact that he didn't have a choice helped to ease his mind in the matter.

"The exciting day arrived. Cronus and Rhea along with Aristaeus, Latona, Cassandra, Apollo and Artemis accompanied Victor to the space port. Prime Nova himself was there to greet them. For Cassandra and Victor it was an emotionally wrenching experience. Only the love and wisdom of the parents saved this from being a totally traumatic experience for the young lovers.

"For their part, Aristaeus and Latona along with Apollo and Artemis, sought to distract Cassandra with conversation about her art and music. Cronus and Prime Nova likewise sought to divert Victor by discussing the scientific aspects of space flight. In this respect, Prime Nova invited the families to come aboard and inspect the scout ship that would transport them to the mother ship. The scout ship was Prime Nova's personal reconnoitering craft. It was saucer-shaped and sixty feet in diameter. This was twice the diameter of the ordinary three man scout ships. It was also far more elaborate in its technology than the smaller craft. The families found this to be very absorbing and for the moment the tensions disappeared. Prime Nova explained the technology and showed them the instrumentation involved in interdimensional spacecraft. As you know, interdimensional type craft are capable of altering their vibration to differing levels which permits them to be either visible or invisible to the three dimensional worlds.

"Little Apollo, who was eight years old, was beside himself with excitement. He begged Prime Nova and Aristaeus to allow him to take this journey with Victor. This was not to be, but they did promise him he could make a similar journey when he was older. As soon as the inspection was completed, farewells were made and the craft departed for the mother ship.

"As they were making the trip from the earth to the mother ship, Prime Nova began explaining to Victor about the various sizes and types of spacecraft that he used aboard the mother ship, and about the function of each. He was trying to prepare Victor for the immensity of the mother craft. He told Victor that the mother ship was presently in orbit beyond the planet now known as Pluto. He described the mother ship as being one hundred miles long and seventy three miles wide by thirty five miles thick. He told Victor that the craft was invulnerable to any known assault and that it was totally self-contained. The name of the craft was Okressa.

"The trip from the earth to Okressa was only a matter of hours. It could have been made faster or slower, depending upon need or whim. Prime Nova wanted to explain and describe the solar system to Victor along the way because he knew of Victor's intense scientific interest and aptitude. This accounted for the particular time span decided upon for the trip. This leg of the journey to Arcturus aboard the scout ship was made in the fourth dimension vibration.

"When they reached the spaceship Okressa, Prime Nova pointed at what appeared to be a planet nearby. He explained to Victor that this was not a planet, but a man-made craft housing the most elaborate computer system in the galaxy. He said that it was in permanent orbit of our solar system sun and that the computer system monitored every happening of any kind that occurred within the solar system. He further explained that such extensive surveillance was necessary to the complete protection of the earth and the solar system. Prime Nova then reminded Victor of the asteroid belt between Mars and Jupiter which had once been the planet Serna, but which had subsequently been destroyed in an atomic war by the human inhabitants. Such an occurrence would never again be allowed. The earth and its solar system were far too important in the Divine Plan to ever again permit such a risk.

"Victor was overawed by the size of Okressa and the man-made planet. No amount of advance warning can actually prepare one for the overwhelming experience of beholding such immense man-made structures. Victor would have been equally awed if they had come in contact with one of the large scout ships. These were ten miles in diameter.

"Prime Nova decided to give Victor a tour of the computer craft before familiarizing him with the Okressa. There would be ample time on the journey to Arcturus to learn all about the Okressa. Rather than an actual physical tour, Prime Nova showed Victor a movie depicting the construction of the man-made planet and the intracacies of the information gathering and surveillance capabilities of the system. The movie, incidentally, was a three-dimensional laser holographic projection. Victor was duly impressed with the scientific technology which made such a huge task possible and was reassured at the protection given the earth and the solar system.

"Before leaving the solar system, Prime Nova decided to tell Victor a bit more about life within this system. First, he told Victor that the sun was hollow. As if this shock was not enough, he quickly told him that the sun was not hot, but cold. Following this, he told Victor that indeed all of the planets are hollow, and that despite appearances to the contrary, all are inhabited by human life in one level of vibration or another. Victor was only shocked for a moment by these astounding revelations. His brilliant intellect coupled with his extraordinary intuition and perceptivity convinced him that if a being such as Prime Nova was telling him these things, there must be substance to the information. He would certainly want to explore these revelations in the future.

CHAPTER 10

"To those scientists in the earth who limit and restrict their thinking, Victor's journey to Arcturus must be relegated to pure fantasy. Fortunately, the limitations of earthman's perceptions and thinking processes do not limit the physical and non-physical realms beyond the earth. The trip from the man-made planet to Arcturus required only one week earth time. This time requirement was not based on the technological capability of the spaceship Okressa, but on the itinerary. We have already told you that time is based upon the motion of one body with relation to another body. We have also stated that the Okressa could travel backward or forward in time—in other words transcend time. When you leave one level of vibration or dimension and move into another, the laws of the prior dimension no longer govern. Whereas in the physical worlds, the speed of light is computed to be the maximum speed attainable, when you enter the fourth dimensional vibration or beyond, the physical speed of light no longer applies. The technological equivalents of the Okressa are vastly beyond the finite limitations of earth thinking. In one day of earth time, the Okressa can journey the equivalent of 200,000,000 years of earth time measure of time and distance. Until your scientists can accommodate such concepts as being within the realm of reasonable possibilities, they will be unable to accept or understand the very theories they seek.

"Victor was continuously overwhelmed by the incomprehensible vastness of the creation. As distant as this journey was in terms of Earth distance, it was but a speck in this sector of space. This sector of space was but a speck in the universe and the universe was but a speck in the total creation. And finally, the creation itself was but a speck in the great void.

"It was so exciting for Victor to explore the self-contained environment of the Okressa. This was an ideal world within itself where every factor from climate to total quality of life was calculated to fulfill the needs of all of its inhabitants. Prime Nova permitted Victor to observe the command center of the great spaceship. The command center provided communication links with all known worlds. On one occasion, Prime Nova spoke to all of his people in the three planet system. This was a television-type broadcast. Young Victor was also permitted to speak to the Novic peoples. He would be a celebrity when he arrived.

"Their destination was the center planet of the three planet system of the great sun star, Arcturus. The Okressa remained in space of course, at a distance of about 100 thousand miles so as not to disrupt the planetary currents. From there they traveled by Prime Nova's personal scout ship to the planet's surface. After all official greetings and ceremonies had taken place over the next several days, Prime Nova assigned Nova Eight, his minister of education, to plan suitable schedules to provide Victor with the diverse experience and training that this journey was designed to impart.

"Some time was spent in traveling around each of the three planets. On each planet Victor met the leaders and some of the ordinary citizens. He invariably found their intellects much more than a match for his own, but even at his age he felt that their lack of emotion evened the score. He felt at ease among these friendly beings, though still a bit self-conscious because of his superior size coupled with his inferior intellect.

"It made him feel better when Nova Eight told him that Earth-type humanoids have the potential for far greater intellect than the Novic people. Nova Eight told Victor that they had studied and analyzed the humans from Earth and from similar worlds for literally thousands of years. In that study they had discovered that human beings have the capability of becoming Gods. They had reasoned that since the human specie was actually a fragmentation of the Eternals, who were God-beings, it logically followed that the human specie must have the same potential as the prototype, the template from which the human sprang. Their subsequent studies, observations and scientific analyses substantiated their hypothesis. Their computer analyses proved beyond a doubt that the human physical body was fully capable of dealing with the most subtle, refined and powerful energies of the universes. They had analyzed not only the physical body, but in conjunction with the mental and spiritual realms, they had also subjected the astral (mental) and etheric (spiritual) bodies to the most exhaustive tests possible to devise. They were convinced beyond a doubt that when all of the possible hook-ups and connections were complete, any man could be a God. They also discovered that the so-called hook-ups and connections were automatic. As any individual attained a certain level of consciousness, it automatically completed certain complex circuits connecting the spiritual centers with the mental, emotional and physical centers. Over thousands of years they had had ample opportunities to observe such great souls as Siddhartha Gautama, Pythagoras, Elihu and others. The changes in the bodies that accompanied the expansion of consciousness were very obvious. The Novic people even reasoned that they could precipitate an expansion of consciousness by technologically making the connections themselves. However, they never tried this because the Great Archangel Michael let it be known that it was not in accordance with the Divine Plan for such interference to be permitted.

"Victor marveled at the knowledge that Nova Eight was revealing to him. Nova Eight continued along this line of explaining the human potential. He reminded Victor of the many myths and legends that have always existed in the Earth and elsewhere concerning the Gods of antiquity. Invariably, these myths spoke of twelve gods and goddesses. So deeply is this knowledge rooted in the souls of men, that wherever men exist, the legends spring to life. The basis of the myths is factual and concerns the twelve Eternal God-beings created before the creation itself. Since the very beginning of time, the Eternals themselves have experienced life on the human scale through the process of fragmentation. Wherever human life has appeared, there have always been dominant persons who have stood out above other men. These dominant beings have been major extensions or fragmentations of the Eternals. Always through the ages, mankind has made heroes, Gods and Goddesses out of its greatest leaders. Each major civilization has somehow managed to produce legends and myths which survive the civilization itself and make of its principle characters the legend-ary Gods of subsequent civilizations.

"It is the process of self-discovery, Victor was told, that enables one to learn and appreciate the truths that Nova Eight was revealing to him. For even though Nova Eight could explain to him the nature of his origin and destiny, only he himself could judge its reality through the process of truly understanding his own self.

"All of Creation and all of life and of living was in actuality a result of the Eternal God-Beings leaving Para-dise on a journey and a mission of gaining knowledge to become like unto the Primal God-Being. Each Eternal is exploring and discovering his/her own self. The method they use is to go within. They accomplish this by fragment-ing their own consciousness in the form of a mini-soul, and then guiding that soul portion into their own immense bodies.

"When viewed from without, the whole of Creation will be seen to be these immense bodies of the Eternals. The Creation which we view from within as stars and planets and gases, is but the atomic level of these huge bodies. From our perspective of being a speck on an electron of a gigantic atom, it is quite impossible to visual-ize the whole of which we are such a minute part. How-ever, if you were to view the Creation from a point in the Great Void beyond the Creation, you would clearly see these God-forms.

"The challenge, Victor was told, was for one to go within their self and discover the same potential which the Eternals were seeking through their consciousnesses. As one does this, the connection is strengthened between the mini-soul consciousness and the total Eternal con-sciousness. Then comes the realization, 'The Father/

Mother God and I are one.' Upon reaching this level of awareness, one then begins to understand all life.

"Nova Eight then told Victor that he was a major extension, or mini-soul, of one of the Eternals. Victor felt comfortable with this revelation. Even for one so young, there was a knowing within him that transcended any doubts he might have had.

"Victor's experience upon the Novic planets was not entirely pleasant from a purely physical viewpoint. The atmosphere was not sufficient to support humans from Earth. Consequently, Victor had to wear special life-support equipment wherever he went. Although the Novic people were accustomed to visitors from other worlds, and they provided such life-support systems within many of their public buildings, still it was inconvenient for an Earth human to function for an extended time in such an environment. It had not been Prime Nova's intention that Victor spend a long time in Arcturus. There were other worlds and galaxies to visit. Before leaving, however, Victor was to learn what the Novic scientists had observed and learned about the human sexual nature.

"Nova Eight knew about Victor's relationship with Cassandra. He knew how very difficult it was for beings with emotions to sever a relationship which brought so much pleasure and fulfillment. While he himself could not experience emotions, he knew from observation the traumatic effect that accompanies the separation of lovers in love. The length of Victor's separation from Cassandra, combined with his partial adjustment to all of the phenomena and wonders of the Novic worlds, served to rekindle the loneliness and hunger that burned within him. Now would be the perfect time for Nova Eight to speak about man's sexual nature. Under the circumstances, the lesson would be most meaningful.

"Nova Eight asked Victor to describe his feelings during the time that he was having his relationship with Cassandra. Victor replied that just being around Cassandra made him feel good. It made him tingle all over. Sometimes it made him dizzy. Always it made him want to merge with her, to couple with her. While joined together in the physical union, it was a bliss beyond compare. He said that for both he and Cassandra, the union imparted a different level of consciousness. He went on to explain that this altered state of consciousness produced a feeling, an emotion, of being 'very close to God.' He did not know how else to describe it. He said it also seemed to open up a deeper flow of creativity, of psychic awareness, of communication with other worlds and dimensions. All things considered, he said it was the only time in his life that he had ever felt complete. He told Nova Eight that each time he and Cassandra had had a union, he had felt incredibly good for several days thereafter, and that when that feeling of balance and well-being began to wear off, the urge to be with Cassandra became obsessive.

"Nova Eight congratulated Victor on his openness and honesty. He assured him that what he had experienced had been beautiful and right. He told him that it would form a good basis for him to be able to understand and relate to what Nova Eight was going to tell him about the sexual nature of human beings.

"For countless thousands of years, the Novic people had been observing humans of many worlds. Without exception, the sexual behavioral patterns in the growth and evolvement of human beings was found to be the same. In the more primitive states, man functioned on a more instinctive level. Then, as man 'advanced' to a more 'civilized' state, to a more intelligent state, there was found the tendency to lose more and more contact with the basic animal instinctive nature. Humanity, as it evolved, was found to be constantly in conflict with itself and with its basic nature. It seemed ironical that as man advanced and became more knowledgeable and more intelligent in so many areas of his life, that the awareness of and understanding of the sexual procreativity and instinctive animal nature should diminish. But this has invariably been the pattern.

"Nova Eight went on to tell Victor that the instinctive nature of man is something that each one should come into accord with. Once you learn and understand that basic functioning process within yourself, you will be far more capable of striking the balanced life that all men seek. Their observations had shown that whenever people grew tired or weak or weary, whenever they entered into a state of depression or melancholy or even self doubt, it was centered around a conflict with that animal nature within each one. Now there are exceptions to this of course. But these exceptions deal with outside factors over which the individual exerts little or no conscious control. When you can harmonize and understand that basic, instinctive portion of yourself that is attuned to the universe, when you can control and direct that natural flow and impulse that is inherent and natural to the animal world, then you can maintain perfect health. Before humanity can truly evolve in any way whatsoever, before there can be the balancing of the mind and the soul and the physical, the physical must be contended with. Nova

Eight reminded Victor of the many individuals in the Earth who contended with what is known as the health process who totally ignore the sexual and procreativity processes which are necessary and vital to health. For instance, there are the doctors and healers who are contending with the physiological and psychological processes. Then there are the nutritionists who are concerned with the dietary needs. Without the basic instinctive animal nature being in balance and accord, no amount of proper nutrition or physical health care is going to produce the required balance.

"There is no set rule for anyone of the human specie. Each is unique. Each has different impulses concerning that instinctive and sexual drive and desire, and each must settle that in their own way and to their own satisfaction. It is not mandatory for any one to follow the dictates of another, for that may not be the system or method that is best suited for you. So therefore, each one must take this within the sanctity of their own inner counsel, and on this level of intense intimacy arrive at a complete understanding about the situation.

"For example, he reminded Victor of the perfect balance and sense of well-being that resulted from Victor's unions with Cassandra. For someone else, that same balance might be achieved through masturbation or through a homosexual relationship. For still others, such a balance might be reached by simply having a platonic relationship. However, in each instance there must be an unhurried approach in dealing with the energies involved. He went on to explain that there are several types of circulation systems in the human body. The only one that is obvious to most humans is the blood circulatory system. The other circulation which science has not understood or even dwelt within properly is the sexual circulation. It is the sexual circulation system that involves the balancing of energies.

"The basic source of all disease in the human physical organism is a misapplication of the mental capabilities within a person concerning the sexual functioning and promotion of those energies and distribution of those energies throughout the body. It has been whispered by various teachers about the energies that move within the body, from one center to the next. All of this energy is sexual in origin. It is the physiological chemical process, which is a sexual process. It is basically electrical. It passes its impulse from one cell to the next. Whenever there is frustration or the energy is not flowing in that circulation properly, when it does not go completely in a counter-clockwise motion throughout the body, from one limb to the next, from one cell to the next, then there is a rise of difficulty within the physical system itself. Each cell of the carbon composed human being needs a con-stant flow of that sexual kenetic energy for it to maintain its immortality status. When that is not arrived at, the cells deteriorate, break down and die. This process is very simple, but it comes with being in harmony with one's own basic nature and instinctive desires and drives. When this secondary sexual circulation flows easily, then there is no congestion and no obstacles or blockages within the body. Where there is a blockage, there is definite sexual frustration. There is a point where this energy is not flow-ing properly. It affects the auric field as well as all of the centers within the body as well as the brain functioning.

"Nova Eight emphasized that basic human creativity is linked to the sexual impulse. He told Victor that human-ity functions at a very low level of the basic mental struc-ture potential. Physically, organically, the mental processes are capable of absorbing all of the knowledge in every library throughout the Earth. All sensory data that passes by in any way conceivable can likewise be easily absorbed. But this again is linked to the sexual circulation.

"Once this sexual balance is maintained or even desired, once it is understood in a technological aspect, then the human mind automatically opens your sensory impulse, automatically increases a thousandfold. Each one is capable mentally and emotionally of producing whatever they desire. This is based upon the energies as they move throughout ones body. The formation of any disease is the blockaging of that energy. All disease is linked to this, and this completely. He stressed that Victor look ever deeper into his human sexuality and the expression of that sexuality, not in the symbolic term, but in the scientific terminology concerning his body.

"Finally, Nova Eight spoke to Victor regarding Victor's desires for psychic ability, of the molding of mind over matter. He stated to Victor that he should observe the lower worlds. When you come to the point of realizing that in the lower worlds, the lower mentalities, (not so much from the mental intellectual standpoint, but from the physical standpoint), as you get lower and lower in the physical realm, you will discover that every living thing has a very definite display of PK ability or the psychic ability that Victor was seeking. In all of the animals and all of the animal kingdoms, they can affect using the PK ability far more easily than mankind. That is because PK is, from the technological standpoint, primitive. It is a primitive ability, but that one basic primitive ability is in direct accord and union with the universal harmony. Paradoxically, as man strives to advance himself, he strives to leave behind the primitive nature within himself, but what he leaves behind is the source of his basic harmony."

At this point I interrupted Diane, just as I had done on a previous occasion when she was relating some very profound ideas. Some questions had occurred to me. I thought that if Diane could answer them it would provide further interesting material for the book. So I asked, "Diane, do you happen to know if the PK energies that Nova Eight was referring to has anything to do with poltergeist activity?"

She replied, "Yes, Joseph. The so-called poltergeist phenomenon of material objects moving or flying about a room is almost invariably linked to the PK energies of young people. I will go further. A great many of your teen-age problems are connected to the mis-channeling of the primitiive instinctive sexual energies. You would find that if society were able to deal with the sexually maturing child in an enlightened way, that most of your teen-age problems would disappear. I think that as our story continues, Joseph, that more of your questions will be answered."

"Then I will withhold any further questions for now, Diane," I replied.

Diane continued. "Nova Eight told Victor that the frustration, discomfort and restlessness that he was now experiencing was a direct result of sexual energy blockage. He reminded Victor that the ecstasy he had experienced with Cassandra was a result of the perfect balancing of the primitive instinctive sexual energy polarities. Since this was a most important consideration in Victor's well-being, a special journey was now planned. When Nova Eight told Victor that they were going to visit another world with human beings, Victor became very excited and eager. He asked if the human beings would look and be like him. Nova Eight responded that they would. He further responded that Victor would meet some lovely young ladies that would help him overcome most of his loneliness and frustration.

"Preparations were completed, temporary farewells spoken and Nova Eight and Victor departed Arcturus for Space Sector N-311 in the Northern Hemisphere of the Universe. The spacecraft chosen for this journey was of the freighter type that regularly transported minerals between worlds. It was rectangular shaped, about one mile in length by one quarter mile wide by one eighth mile thick. The purpose in utilizing this craft was partially to instruct Victor in the economics and mechanics of space trade and partially because this particular craft was already scheduled to make the trip to the planet which was their destination.

CHAPTER 11

"The planet Reath was similar to Earth in so many ways. The essential differences lie in the degree of enlightenment of its inhabitants. If you were to describe either planet, your description would come close to describing the other. Even the solar system of which it was a part was almost identical. The major difference would have been in the appearance of the night skies. You would not recognize any of the constellations familiar to the Galaxy of the Milky Way.

"Reath had a moderate amount of visitation from beings of other planets and worlds, so this visit was not unusual. What was unusual was to have a human visitor from another sector of space so far removed. Such an occasion was of planetary interest. Accordingly, Victor would receive a reception similar to his welcome on Arcturus.

"Upon arrival, Nova Eight, Victor and the Captain of the spacecraft took a small shuttlecraft to the planet's surface where they were met by Endymion, Minister of Education of Planet Reath. Unlike Earth, Reath had long since advanced to the point of unification of all peoples upon the planet. It was a physical planet of surpassing beauty and freedom from the kind of strife that still characterized most levels of society in the Earth. Reath was, in fact, the idealized version of what life in the physical worlds should be like. It was not a planet that just anyone could visit. It was not a planet that just anyone could incarnate into. It was reserved for those souls who were well advanced in their evolution through the physical worlds. A soul was allowed to incarnate on Reath for only one lifetime. Life here was so ideal, so fulfilling, that to remain here beyond one lifetime was to make returning to the other physical worlds beyond enduring. Reath was a world without struggle or strife, a world balanced with goals—balanced with creativity and promise and hope. It was a world without unnecessary death or suffering or sorrow, a world where all living beings lived harmoniously and man enjoyed the act of living, creating and growing; exploring the countless billions and billions of mysteries and promises and beautiful things. It was a world without decay, but with only reward, with only promise—where not one living thing needed to suffer, not one living thing needed to be denied anything, but all things worked and strove together for a common goal of beauty. It was a world where each beautiful thing always strove to make more beautiful things for the appreciation and for the benefit of other beautiful things—where there was no darkness nor strife, no shadow nor loneliness, no sorrow, no tears of sadness—only love, laughter and living, only growth and untold avenues of growing, unknown and untold beauty and benevolence, a world of peace and harmony."

"It sounds to me, Diane, as if you are describing Paradise," I said.

"In many ways it is Paradise, Joseph," she said, and then continued. "It is not the ultimate Paradise of which the Great Archangel Michael speaks, but it is the ultimate physical world in the Creation. That is why no one is allowed to incarnate there for more than one lifetime. It is meant to show advanced souls what can be attained in the physical worlds. It is meant to inspire and refresh those souls who have grown weary in the long struggle for self realization. It is meant to reconnect one to the level of their deepest love, to their deepest goals, aspirations and desires. It is meant to refresh and reinspire one to complete that final step that separates them from the rediscovery of their true identity.

"Into this marvelous world Victor was brought to catch a glimpse of Paradise and hold these memories in his consciousness for the remainder of his life.

"Endymion escorted Nova Eight and Victor to the home of Nestor, ruler of Planet Reath. Nestor explained to Victor the things that I have already described to you pertaining to Reath and its purpose. He told Victor of his own incarnations in Planet Earth plus the fact that he would be returning there soon to complete his own evolutionary growth. He then told Endymion that Victor would be his guest during the remainder of his stay on Reath. Endymion had already invited Nova Eight to be his guest until he returned to Arcturus. Nova Eight and Endymion would have much to share concerning their roles as Ministers of Education of their respective worlds.

"Nestor introduced Victor to his family which consisted of his wife, Berenice, and their daughter Protogenia. Both mother and daughter were women of extraordinary beauty in a land where beauty was rampant. His first gaze upon Protogenia made Victor completely forget about Cassandra for the moment. Victor could not at first believe his reaction to Protogenia. When introduced to her, the moment he touched her hand he was rendered almost speechless by the effect of her vibration blending with his own. There was a similar effect upon Protogenia. All of this was readily observed by Nestor and Berenice. However, it was not observed with disapproval, for this was a land of enlightenment where such things were readily understood. Victor and Protogenia were the same age, the same level of intelligence and similar in their soul growth and evolvement.

"After becoming acquainted with Victor, mother and daughter excused themselves so that Nestor could meet privately with Victor. Nestor wanted to prepare Victor so that his visit would be most fruitful and productive. He proceeded to describe Reath to Victor as I have already described it to you, as to its purpose and place in the scheme of the Divine Plan. He also described in some detail what Victor could expect to experience in everyday living in this environment. Knowing of the intense attraction between Victor and Protogenia, he explained the philosophy governing the relationship between male and female on the Planet Reath. In an environment of such love and high ideals, it was only natural for intense attractions to manifest frequently between men and women. Such attractions were not based solely upon the primitive instinctive nature responding to the stimuli of lust. The enlightened soul finds it quite easy and natural to love openly and freely. This is because the enlightened soul has learned that love is the only reason to live at all. Such a soul recognizes at once the beauty and the divinity within each other soul. Such a soul also recognizes that no genuine love is ever wrong, and that however such love chooses to manifest itself between two individuals is alright. The sense of responsibility that is inherent in the soul of an enlightened one precludes such a one from misusing or abusing another.

"Victor correctly concluded from this explanation that Nestor was giving his approval to whatever relationship might develop between he and Protogenia. He was therefore understandably anxious to be with Protogenia.

"During the evening meal discussion centered around the similarities and differences between the planets Reath and Earth. Nestor offered to Victor his rather startling concepts of the nature of the creation. Much to Victor's surprise, these concepts were quite similar to those expressed to him previously by Nova Eight. Nestor, too, believed that the creation was in reality the actual bodies of the gods. Furthermore, he believed that Reath and Earth were the two most important planets and worlds in all of the creation. Nestor stated unequivocally that every thing that exists has life and a certain level of intelligence and knowing. He also stated that every life is activated and sustained by a divine essence which he called 'life force.' His belief was that in the heart of every living thing, there was a primal atom that contained this life force. He said that in the left ventricle of the heart of every human being, there exists this primal atom which is the creative and sustaining life force essence. He then stated that he believed that the same principle stemmed from God and that the essence of life force of God was focused in the solar system that contained the Planet Earth. It was his belief that Earth was the primal electron in the primal atom of the left ventricle of the heart of God. This planet Earth represented the raw potential of the dream of God for the physical creation. Reath, on the other hand, was the primal electron in the primal atom of the right ventricle of the heart of God. Reath represented the dream, the goal and the ideal which Earth was some day destined to manifest. Reath was the will of God of what man in the Earth was to become. Earth was the free will of man going through the painful process of good and evil while learning how to become the Gods of tomorrow. Reath existed to remind man of his goals in the creation. Reath existed as the pattern and the prototype of what Earth and man were to become. In order for the plan to succeed, Earth must reach the perfection of Reath through the free choice of man. Such a triumph can only come about through man's victory over both good and evil. Such a triumph can only manifest if man discovers himself and his God nature. For man to discover himself, he must first learn what it means to go within. Man must learn that he is a clone of God, that he is made in the image and likeness of God and that he has the potential and destiny of becoming a God.

"All religions, all philosophies and all mythologies have actually been based upon getting these concepts across to mankind. In the process, the goals become hidden and buried beneath a mountain of man-made confusion, doubt, theology, institutionalization, and mystery.

"Poor Victor! The deeper conversation became, the more difficulty he had in coping with the magical vibrations of Protogenia. He was interested in what Nestor was saying, but there was a severe conflict between his mental curiosity and his total bodily and emotional needs. Nestor was certainly not unaware of this inner struggle. Nor was Berenice, his wife. Together they arose and excused themselves from the young couple, leaving Victor and Protogenia to discover for themselves the nature of those energies that were impelling them.

"Protogenia invited Victor to her room where they

could talk undisturbed. They did very little talking that evening. By some unspoken mutual consent, they mostly just sat side by side absorbing the feelings of being in the close presence of each other. It was a new and totally exhilarating experience for both of them. The interaction of their electromagnetic energies produced an exuberance that was perfectly moderated by a joyful serenity. They sat up until well past the middle of the night. They did not want to part then, but they were fearful that if they did not get enough sleep it would interfere with the busy schedule planned for the morrow. They needn't have been concerned. The balancing effect that they had produced in each other precluded the need for much sleep that night.

"The days that followed were busy ones. It really was exciting for Victor to learn and discover the things about Reath that man of Earth would someday have to achieve. Victor was certainly aware that he had some responsibility to communicate some of these goals to mankind in the Earth. And as for Protogenia, it was equally exciting to be told about the conditions in Earth that were so different. She knew that her next lifetime would be spent there.

"Victor and Protogenia were escorted throughout the planet by Endymion and Nova Eight. Victor was absolutely amazed at the level of psychic ability that seemed natural for everyone. In thinking back to his first night with Protogenia, he now realized that the reason that they did not talk aloud very much was because they were so busy communicating silently. He had not fully realized at the time that they were exchanging thoughts telepathically. In the days that had followed, it had become more obvious as Protogenia had begun verbalizing many of the unspoken thoughts which he had had that night.

"One of the things which Victor had observed as they traveled about the planet was the almost complete absence of infants. When he began to realize how unusual this was in comparison to life in the Earth, he asked Endymion for an explanation.

"Endymion explained that the usual process of begetting and raising children in Reath was completely different than Earth. Customarily, children of Reath did not arrive through the female birth canal. Although it was physiologically possible for birth of children to take place in this so-called normal manner, it was not generally considered desirable or convenient to subject oneself to the fertilization, gestation process. On Reath, over ninety five percent of all parents chose alternative methods. The most common method was to have your child's future body gestated in the laboratory until it reached the point of maturity that was agreeable to the parents and the incoming soul. When that point was reached, a beautiful ceremony was participated in by parents and friends while the soul of the new arrival entered the prepared body. In this way, the mother was spared all of the discomforts of pregnancy, and the incoming child was spared the discomforts of teething, bowel training, learning to articulate and control the motor responses of the body, etc. The result was a very happy and mutually satisfying experience. The newly incoming souls could start their new incarnation as precocious children who had been spared the tortures that accompany birth and weening in the Earth. There were absolutely no unwanted children. All family situations were by prior agreement.

"The alternative method of procreation was reserved for those advanced souls who were capable of manipulating and utilizing the sexual energies. When this point is reached, it is possible to use the mind power to materialize the sexual energies into matter. When parenting is accomplished in this manner, both of the parents manipulate the energies from the physical dimension while the incoming soul controls the process from the non-physical end. The result is the formation of a new physical body in a matter of minutes.

"Endymion reminded Victor that such methods of begetting children did not interfere with the normal and frequent sexual energy exchange between couples. Quite the contrary was true. The removal of the act of procreating children from the sexual union of two souls actually enhanced the relationship and the communication process. He said that in planets like Earth there was often uncertainty and tension blocking the communication between lovers because of the possibility of unwanted pregnancy. On Reath, unwanted pregnancies did not occur. Furthermore, parents had a full range of choices as to method of child procreation. If a couple chose to go through the process of pregnancy and gestation, they were free to do so, but the need did not appeal to very many. This was because all had had many prior incarnations in physical worlds where they had no choice. They simply did not require the experience or the pain involved.

"Because of the degree to which telepathic communication was practiced in Reath, parents were aware of the life goals of new souls before they incarnated. Such matters were freely discussed telepathically. In this way it was determined if the incoming soul's needs and desires could best be provided through the selected parents.

"Victor was fascinated with all of this information. He told Endymion that scientists in Atlantis had already succeeded in laboratory experiments of gestating fetuses. He told Endymion that such experiments had generated great controversy in some circles. He also mentioned that some in the Earth were making good progress in developing their psychic skills. He asked if there were any particular methods that were more effective than others in aiding psychic development.

"Endymion replied that the sexual energy exchange provided one of the best known methods for enhancing the psychic capabilities. He reminded Victor of the effects of being in the presence of someone of the same vibration—of how such a presence affected the emotions, the mental processes and the physical reactions. The interaction of the sexual energies heightens the sensory response. This involves not only the physical senses, but the entire extrasensory spectrum as well. The next time you experience this vibratory compatibility, he suggested to Victor, remember to remain silent and open your consciousness fully to telepathic communication. This statement by Endymion led Victor's thoughts invariably to Protogenia. He could not wait to be alone with her again.

"That evening Protogenia and Victor arranged to be alone. Victor asked her if she had ever had a physical sexual union with anyone. She told him that while she had had several non-physical unions of an intense sexual nature, she had had only one physical coupling. That had taken place only months before when friends of her parents had visited with their teen-age son from the other side of the planet. She said it had been an interesting experience, but that the attraction hadn't been strong enough to produce the desired effect. She then told Victor that the attraction which she felt toward him was the strongest she had ever felt. Victor admitted that just being with Protogenia caused a surge in emotion that only Cassandra had ever produced before. They agreed to sit quietly together as before and be as receptive as possible.

"It was only a matter of moments when both Victor and Protogenia felt a rush of energy which instantly altered their consciousness. They looked at one another in startled amazement, then closing their eyes, they both lay back to allow the communication to develop. So strong and pleasurable and pervading was the sensation that gripped Victor, that he felt certain that he would have an orgasm. Protogenia was experiencing the identical sensations. For a long time they both immersed themselves in the rapture produced by their intertwining auras. Eventually Protogenia reached over and touched Victor on the hand. This physical touch produced another, stronger surge of energy which resulted in a spontaneous mutual embrace. The embrace in turn sparked an explosion of consciousness that instantly opened their minds to the memories of their pasts!

"Victor could hardly believe the vision of his own past that was parading before his consciousness. What he saw at that moment was an excerpt from his life as Victor during his first Atlantean incarnation. He was age fifteen. He saw himself having his first sexual union with his girl friend, Victoria. He knew then that Victoria was Protogenia. Victoria had later become his wife in that lifetime and the two of them had been extremely close and compatible. This was the basis for the powerful attraction that drew them together now. Protogenia's vision was paralleling that of Victor. Without speaking, each knew what the other was witnessing from the past. The realization of this only further intensified the experience.

"With this experience, Victor now better understood the power of the electro-chemical sexual energies to unlock the doorways of the various levels of consciousness. Now he could relate more intelligently to Endymion's advice regarding psychic development. The truly incredible thing to Victor was the total fulfillment that resulted from this exchange. Here, indeed, was an unbelievably satisfying and complete sexual blending without the physical joining. The energizing, balancing and harmonizing effects were as complete and total as any physical coupling could produce.

"In the days that followed, Victor and Protogenia continued to relate in the same way. They never did attempt a physical union. The sensitivity of their psychic abilities continued to increase. Their intuitive levels rose dramatically. They reached the point of full telepathic connection with each other. Coincidentally, the time had arrived for Victor to return to Arcturus. The thought of leaving Protogenia and the heavenly planet of Reath produced the same feeling of desolation that he had felt when he knew he had to leave Cassandra. Having had this experience, however, made him realize that the potential existed for similar relationships in other worlds and places.

"Victor and Protogenia agreed that they wanted to experience a physical union before parting. That night they began their exchange by gazing deeply and lovingly into each others' eyes. The usual rush of energy enfolded them. As they adjusted to the thrill and ecstasy of this love blanket of divine vibrations, they simultaneously extended a hand to each other. The heightened effect of this touch led again to a spontaneous physical embrace. While they were measuring the bliss of this further intimacy, their bodies were automatically responding by completing the intimacy of a full physical union. This final contact propelled them into a state of sublime consciousness and complete emotional bliss. They remained in this state for perhaps two hours. In terms of expansion of consciousness and sheer experiencing, two hours in this mood would have the equivalent of one or more lifetimes of dedicated pursuit of knowledge and feeling. While in this embrace, all of Victor's past Earth incarnations flashed before him. At the same time he caught glimpses of himself in the mental realm prior to this life, planning the various episodes of this life. He saw quite clearly what he intended to accomplish in this lifetime. Protogenia likewise witnessed flashbacks of her Earth incarnations and realized the importance that her lifetime in Reath would have in the future history of Earth. They both knew beyond a doubt that even though they would be parting physically, the telepathic bond between them would not be broken by the distance to Earth. This knowingness was a great comfort to them and made their final hours together very warm and happy.

"Nova Eight and Victor returned to Arcturus aboard an interdimensional spacecraft provided by Nestor. While this was by no means the end of Victor's experiences in space, we must shift now to Cassandra."

"I can't help but notice, Diane," I said, "that your descriptions of the sex life of Victor are becoming much more vivid and interesting. For someone so young, he was really learning how to get it on, as they say."

"Well Joseph," she responded, "a primary purpose of our story is to document the progression of a soul from one life to the next. A most important part of that progression is the awakening of a soul to the full potential of its sexual nature. If we can get across the reality of the deep emotional impact of sex upon the soul, then it will bring about a greater understanding of the best use of sex to mankind. Michael is going to speak to you now."

CHAPTER 12

"If you will recall, Joseph," said Michael, "I had mentioned to you briefly about Cassandra having decided to devote her life's work to the arts, music and development of her psychic abilities. I also mentioned about the little group of six people that joined together seeking the answers to life's deeper mysteries. Finally, I told you a bit about the culture and technology of Atlantis at that particular time. As Diane was relating to you some of Victor's life, she flashed back to the experiences of Cassandra and Victor growing from early childhood to the age of thirteen, when they parted. I will now fill you in on Cassandra's life from age thirteen when Victor left for Arcturus, until Victor's return at age nineteen.

"Aristaeus (Cassandra's father) had consulted with his close friend, Cronus (Victor's father), concerning the parting of Victor and Cassandra. There was no way to prevent a degree of trauma to both young people. However, it was their intent to minimize the trauma as much as possible and in as constructive a way as possible. Victor's space journey was the perfect solution to divert Victor's attention from his emotional pain and direct his thinking and focus to learning those truths which would be invaluable in his future role as ruler of Atlantis. For Cassandra, another

119

kind of journey was planned. Whereas Victor's journey was one into outer space, Cassandra's journey was to be to the inner spaces of Earth.

"Here we go again, Michael," I said. "First your story deals in mythology. Then you speak of Lemuria and Atlantis, the two great ancient, but unproven, civilizations of Earth. Then you take Victor on an outer space journey to other galaxies. Now you're talking about the inner spaces of Earth. How do you expect anyone to believe all of these things?"

"As I told you before, Joseph," said Michael, "It's not so important that people believe all of the facts. Intelligent people are looking for answers. We are providing many answers. We believe that many people will search their hearts as they read this story, and that many of the things we speak about will have meaning for them and will help them. However, in the final analysis let me say this. Our story is true. Truth has a way of reaching the soul of the seeker, even though the outer garments may temporarily distract the gaze.

"The Planet Earth holds more secrets than man dares dream. What I tell you now is only one of those great secrets. You remember that Prime Nova told Victor that the Sun and all planets are hollow. In the hollow of the Earth are great civilizations. I am not going to speak of these at this time. I am going to tell you that in addition to the hollow interior of the Earth, there are also a few great city civilizations in the crust of the Earth. I am going to tell you of one such place.

"The entire continent of South America has been preserved for this day and time. It contains more secrets than the rest of the Earth. Hidden in and beneath those great jungles are the answers to many mysteries and puzzles that have titillated and perplexed man for centuries. The city of which I speak is located beneath those jungles. I will not say exactly where for many and obvious reasons, because the city exists to this day. Ever since man has been experimenting with and experiencing life on the Earth, man has also been in this underground city. Mankind and life in this city differs from life on the Earth just as much as life on Reath differs from life on Earth. In a philosophical sense, you could say that this underground city represents the goodness in Earth. Deep within the heart and soul of every man there is goodness and purity and love. You do not have to look elsewhere for it. One does not have to go to Reath to find that perfection to which good men aspire in the Earth. Cassandra would be taken to this underground city, and there she would learn and experience many of the things that Victor had traveled to a far and distant galaxy to acquire.

For convenience, I am going to call this underground city Ciudad de Oro. There has seldom been a time when one or more of the citizens of Ciudad de Oro was not walking the Earth among men of the outer Earth. They would not be recognized by anyone but the most psychic as being different, for their appearance is the same as yours. The only thing that distinguishes them in a physical way is the ring they wear. Spiritually, they are very pure of heart and in a quiet way they do much to help mankind on the Earth.

"As great spiritual leaders and beings, Cronus and Aristaeus had learned of this city and its inhabitants. Occasionally, they were visited by them. On one occasion, Cronus and Aristaeus had each been invited to visit Ciudad de Oro and had done so. It was during the time of Victor and Cassandra's affair that Aristaeus was again visited by one such being whose name was Janus.

"Aristaeus discussed with Janus the possibility of Cassandra visiting Ciudad de Oro. Janus was very receptive. Although visitations by outsiders were quite rare and were limited to highly evolved souls, Janus knew that Cassandra was qualified and would be welcome by the ruling council. Accordingly, arrangements were made for the journey to take place as soon as Victor departed for Arcturus.

"Of course, Cassandra was consulted in the matter beforehand. She was understandably excited, just as Victor was excited about his journey to Arcturus. She could not help but wonder and speculate what life must be like in an underground city. The idea seemed strange to her. Her own life on the Earth's surface was so idyllic that she could not imagine a life underground to compare in beauty and fulfillment. Being so artistic and sensitive, she began to feel sorry for all the things that must be missing in the lives of the underground inhabitants.

"Her father, Aristaeus, had never discussed Ciudad de Oro with her before now. Nor had she known before now where Janus was from. Neither Aristaeus or Janus intended to spoil the surprises in store for her by revealing anything prematurely.

"The day following Victor's departure for Arcturus, Janus and Cassandra left for South America aboard an aircraft. The aircraft would not take Janus and Cassandra directly to the entrance to Ciudad de Oro. Instead, they would fly to a small city about twenty miles from Ciudad de Oro and walk the remaining distance through the jungle. For reasons which I have already indicated, no one else must know or have any suspicion of the existance of the underground world.

"Upon reaching their destination, Janus announced to Cassandra that they were at the entrance. Cassandra looked around and told Janus that she did not see any entrance to anything. As she was speaking, she suddenly became aware that the ground they were standing upon was gradually sinking below the surface of the surrounding ground. A very cleverly disguised elevator was lowering them into the secret world. The ground they had been standing upon was but a platform. It could have been a magic carpet judging from Cassandra's reactions to the dazzling city they emerged into. She was in no way prepared for the brilliant spectacle that confronted her.

"If anything in the Earth could have been calculated to take Cassandra's mind from constant thoughts of Victor, this world of wonder was certainly that thing. The sensitive soul and nature of Cassandra reacted immediately and strongly to the vibrations of love and beauty that surrounded her. She gasped in wonderment. Speechless, she gazed at Janus as if to ask for an explanation of how this could be.

"Perceiving her unasked question, Janus proceeded to tell Cassandra the incredible story of this world within a world. In reality, this vast underground city was actually a huge craft from another world and another time. Millions of years ago when it came time for mankind to begin experiencing life and evolution in the Earth, human beings from distant galaxies were guided to this planet. They experimented with various life forms to determine that which would be most fitting and adaptable for the human species. When they had decided upon the appropriate form, they mutated existing primitive forms to the point where they would be suitable for occupancy by the human soul. Gradual experimentation over millions of years led to the form that would be ideal for the human vehicle in which to attain Godhood. This development was always under the overall direction of the Great Archangel Michael in cooperation with the Brotherhood of the White Light. At a given point in this development, it was decided to establish this great city as a sanctuary for the archetypal man who would eventually blanket the Earth.

"At that time the Earth had no technology to construct such a sanctuary. It was therefore decided to build this special craft in a distant galaxy where such technology existed, and then fly the craft to Earth and conceal it where it is now."

"Do you think, Michael," I interjected, "That this part of your story is going to have any credibility with our future readers?"

"I don't know why not, Joseph," he replied. "If they can accept the plausibility of the rest of our story, this part should not present any problem. After all, your own Earth scientists have been planning to erect bases on your moon for years. If it were technologically possible for them at this point to prefabricate a complete moon base and fly it to the moon, I'm sure they would do so. Well, in fact, it is technologically possible for them even now. Basically, it's only a matter of economics and logistics and politics that prevents it.

"At the time when this great spacecraft was built and brought to the Earth, it was the most practical solution to the problem. In any event, Cassandra did not have any problem accepting this reality. Within the technological context of those days in Atlantis, such a project was very feasible.

"At first, the craft was settled into a huge valley which had been excavated for the purpose. Originally, the upper surface of the craft was visible. Many centuries later, it was decided to cover the surface with soil and natural vegetation in order to permanently conceal it. The dimensions of the craft are fifteen miles on each side by five miles deep. It is totally self-contained, even to its own weather system. The materials of which it is built are not subject to the same level of corrosion or deterioration as are Earth elements. Consequently, all systems within the craft are still viable and functioning to this day.

"Although it is not part of our story, Joseph, you may be interested to know that there are other such craft on and in the Earth. There are others in the jungles of South America, there are some beneath the oceans and there are many in the great mountain ranges of the Earth. They do not all serve the same purpose, nor are they from the same source. Some are large, though none as large as Ciudad de Oro. Some are interdimensional and some are purely physical. There are a number of craft in the atmosphere around Earth at any given time. Those, too, are of many sizes, shapes, dimensions, purposes and sources.

"I know that there are many people in the Earth who would feel most uncomfortable to learn about this. It would make them feel very insecure and threatened. However, when you consider that Earth is the primary focal point for the entire Divine Plan, it is only natural for those of many worlds to be interested. It seems to be the nature of unevolved man to take a very proprietary interest in wherever he is and to reject as an unwanted outsider anyone he doesn't know.

"By the time Janus finished explaining to Cassandra the story behind the construction of the underground world, they had reached one of the areas of open space within the craft that was devoted to agriculture and horticulture. Cassandra was already exhilarated from the experience of just being in this environment. To behold the wonders of the agricultural and horticultural achievements of this world within a world caused her to burst out in song. The delight that filled her sensitive soul to witness the ultimate rapport between man and animal and the plant kingdom was more than she could contain. After all, her father, Aristaeus, was the greatest known horticulturist on the Earth, and he had instilled into her a great knowledge and appreciation of these things. Yet here before her was the greatest example that man could conceive in these fields of endeavor. Tears flooded her eyes as she began to communicate telepathically with the little beings of the plant and animal worlds.

"Janus told her that her father, Aristaeus, had learned many things in this city which had benefitted the world above. He told her that she, also, had many things to look forward to. He had wanted Cassandra to see these wonders before he showed her anything else, knowing it would make her feel at home. Next he took her to meet the ruler and the Minister of Agriculture and Horticulture. Cassandra seemed surprised when she was introduced to Melissa. She was not expecting the Minister of Agriculture and Horticulture to be a woman. There were no women on the ruling council of Atlantis at this time. When she met Heracles, the ruler, she knew she was meeting the most learned and powerful man in the Earth.

"Arrangements had been made for Cassandra to be the guest of Melissa during the first part of her stay in Ciudad de Oro. Melissa was married to Arcas, who was Minister of Technology and who was also a master of agricultural science. They had two children. The eldest was a son, Dionysus, age fifteen. The other was a daughter, Euterpe, who was Cassandra's age.

"Dionysus possessed the same absorbing interest in horticulture as did his gifted mother. He was constantly experimenting with the yield and hybridization of various plants. His specialty was grapes. He had succeeded in producing three hybrid varieties of such singular and superior properties, that when they were blended together in the fermentation process, they resulted in the finest wine ever made. So although he had not yet reached full adulthood, he had already achieved great fame among the cities' many wine lovers. In a city where precocity was the standard among children, Dionysus was clearly a genius. In addition to his intellect, he also displayed the humility and strength of character that distinguished the children of this world. He was indeed a handsome and appealing young man. And judging from the way he returned Cassandra's look when they were introduced, he was quite interested in Cassandra. It was obvious that the attraction was mutual.

"Euterpe was a great deal like Cassandra. Besides both being the same age, they also shared musical and artistic abilities and interests. Euterpe sang and wrote lyric poetry. Often, like Cassandra, the words would flow extemporaneously from her lips as she sang the musical notes that were springing from her heart. She loved to play the flute. She was frequently to be found in the bountiful fields playing to the little beings who responded with dancing and joyous laughter. Her fascination for and adeptness in psychic ability insured that she and Cassandra would spend many interesting hours together.

"Altogether, if Cassandra could have invented an environment that would allow her to be distracted from constant thoughts of Victor, she would have selected a setting such as this. The first week was spent in an almost continuous touring of this great city. There were two primary levels within the five mile depth. The first level was utilized chiefly as a rural area devoted to agriculture and horticulture. The second level was devoted mainly to the city itself and to the type of urban life characteristic of such an advanced society. In addition to these two primary levels, there were many other smaller levels to insure variety within the environment and to provide for such other facilities as were required in order to be self-contained.

"During this first week, Cassandra reacted well to the therapy. Euterpe had been assigned to guide her in her orientation to the cultural aspects of Ciudad de Oro. This exposed Cassandra to those pursuits in which she was most deeply interested in a vocational and cultural way. With Euterpe to guide her, she was assured of a knowledgeable exposure. They toured the museums, the theaters, the shops. They browsed through the arts and crafts centers, the education center and the decorator studios. They visited the smartest coutures, cafes, jewelers, parks and recreation centers. From dawn till bedtime they occupied themselves with the fun activities that delight children of all ages. Fleeting thoughts of Victor kept flashing before Cassandra, but it was not a painful thing.

"During this first week, Dionysus managed to be around whenever Euterpe and Cassandra were home. He tried to act as if he was preoccupied, but he fooled no one. Everyone was too perceptive to be deceived by his pretended nonchalance. He was clearly captivated by Cassandra. This in spite of the fact that he was extremely popular and could be with virtually anyone he chose in Ciudad de Oro. Cassandra was equally spellbound with Dionysus. She could barely wait until the following week when it would be Dionysus' turn to indoctrinate her into those areas of his expertise.

"Finally Dionysus' turn arrived. That morning the entire house was charged with a pleasant tension. One could almost feel the excitement and anticipation churning within both Cassandra and Dionysus. The air at breakfast was electrical. Everyone was aware of the reason. Arcas casually asked Dionysus his plans for the day. This relaxed everyone as they listened to Dionysus discuss several ideas of his proposed itinerary. His strongest impression was that they should begin their tour in the laboratory where he conducted most of his experiments in hybridization. From there he felt they would probably go into the fields. He said they might well spend two or more days in the fields observing the great variety of plant and animal life under cultivation. This talk of fields brought visions to Cassandra of her last days with Victor. Such talk was not conducive to lessening her sense of expectancy of being alone with Dionysus.

"Finally Dionysus and Cassandra departed together. For the first time they were alone. As they headed for the laboratory in the family hovercraft, the effect of their energies upon each other produced an emotional high for both of them. Consequently, they did not attempt to carry on a conversation. Rather, they just enjoyed the feeling of being alone together for the first time.

"The laboratory was extensive in scope and many people worked there. It was obvious that Dionysus knew his way around and that he was highly respected by everyone in spite of his youthfulness. He was really quite professional and scientific in his approach to his avocation. Many eyes greeted the young couple everywhere they went. The people of this world were mostly quite sensitive and they readily discerned the magnetic energies flowing between the two. Cassandra had not spent much time in the laboratories in Atlantis. She had preferred the beauties of the gardens and outdoors. But under Dionysus guidance and instruction, she was gaining a new perspective and appreciation of how the laboratory augments the productivity and variety of the fields. She did not have to feign an interest. Dionysus' enthusiasm in his work made her excited. He showed her a new variety of grain that had been theorized by their computer system which was now being hybridized in the laboratory. This one grain would provide the whole spectrum of basic nutrients essential to good health and would have a powerful healing effect on the body of anyone who was physically ill. Dionysus told Cassandra that it was Prime Nova's scientists who had suggested the concept for such a food. Cassandra would be sure to tell her father, Aristaeus, about this discovery if it was successful.

"At first Cassandra was surprised to learn that Prime Nova was known by the people of Ciudad de Oro. Dionysus told her that they had been in contact with the Novic people for thousands of years, and had worked in cooperation with them in many ways. There was an expecially close relationship between Arcas and Prime Nova.

"Before the young couple realized it, the day had passed and they had not completed their tour of the laboratory. They would have to begin the second day in the lab before taking to the fields. Having gained a new and deeper appreciation for the technical end of horticulture, Cassandra was filled with great satisfaction and looked forward to the completion of her instruction.

CHAPTER 13

"The following morning found the young couple at the breakfast table before anyone else arrived. Arcas joined them just as they were finishing their meal. He was curious as to when Dionysus planned to show Cassandra the technological systems connected with Ciudad de Oro. Dionysus informed him that this was planned after their tour of the fields and gardens was completed. He stated that would take another three or four days. Arcas then requested that the three of them travel together on that day so that he could explain some of the capabilities of their new technologies to Cassandra. Dionysus agreed.

"With that the young couple again headed for the lab. Today there was a greater excitement around them. The invisible energies were stronger; the hunger they were feeling towards one another more compelling. One does not ignore such forces. One cannot. Nor are such powerful drives readily sublimated. However, to the credit of Cassandra and Dionysus, they did manage to concentrate their focus and attention on completing the tour of the laboratories. This they accomplished by early afternoon, and then they took to the fields with a picnic lunch.

"Dionysus selected his favorite spot for their picnic. It was beside a most picturesque stream that gurgled energetically along the beautifully contoured landscape. The surrounding area alternated between kneehigh grassy meadow filled with blooming wild flowers, and clumps of trees gracefully arranged to frame the whole idyllic setting. They spread a blanket on the grassy embankment a few feet from the stream in the shelter of a dense cluster of trees. Although hungry for lunch due to an early breakfast, their hunger for each other superceded the unpacking of their picnic. A mutual contact of the eyes of this sensitive couple in this conducive setting produced an impulsive embrace that surprised and overwhelmed them both. They would not eat for awhile. They laid back in each others' arms and filled their minds with the bliss of this long awaited moment.

"Cassandra's thoughts drifted to Victor. Although she loved him very, very much and missed him terribly, this did not diminish the thrill of being in Dionysus' arms. She realized that she loved Dionysus also, and that there was no conflict in loving both. She knew that she and Victor were not to be together in this life and she wondered if Dionysus was to be her mate.

"Dionysus was trying to understand what it was about Cassandra that affected him differently than all the other girls he had known. He knew from the moment he first saw her that she was special. He knew that he could not wait to be alone with her and now he was.

"They both wanted to talk, but the need and desire to silently nourish the glorious exchange of energies prevailed. Without realizing it was happening, they both fell asleep in each others' arms. After awhile they awoke simultaneously with huge appetites and quickly ate their lunch. When they finished, Dionysus asked Cassandra if she had ever had a physical sexual union before. She told him of her relationship with Victor which had so recently ended. He then asked her if she had ever experienced cosmic sex. She replied that she and Victor had both undergone altered states of consciousness several times during their unions, if that's what he meant by cosmic sex. Dionysus told her that an altered state of consciousness in itself is not any evidence of cosmic sex, but that a union that climaxes with an orgasm accompanied by uncontrollable laughter is a certain sign that one has broken the barrier. Having had her curiosity aroused, she asked Dionysus if he had experienced cosmic sex himself. He replied that he had not. He told Cassandra that Arcas had explained it to him, and that Arcas had also explained the most likely circumstances under which the experience can occur.

"From Arcas description of the process, Dionysus told Cassandra that he would like to try it with her. He said that all of the essential elements seemed to be there. They both felt a strong love for each other. There was an intense and extremely pleasant reaction whenever their auras merged, as their electro-magnetic biological currents interacted. Furthermore, they were both intelligent, perceptive and well-balanced. Cassandra agreed that she would like to try and attain the cosmic sex experience. They decided they would make love tomorrow in this spot.

"They spent the remainder of the afternoon in the vineyards and in the processing plant before returning home. It was in the processing plant that Cassandra learned of the methods of preserving the freshness and nutritive value of produce without the use of harmful chemicals or other additives. The chemists had developed an inert liquid that could be diluted with water when washing the produce. This left a fine film of the inert liquid covering the produce which effectively blocked out most of the oxygen for up to ten days, thus insuring freshness and wholesomeness. Produce that was to be stored for longer periods was dried and sealed in airtight containers in a mixture of relatively inert gases.

"You can understand that at this point, Joseph, Cassandra was not completely engrossed by all this information. She was paying attention, but her mind was strongly on the morrow," Michael said to me.

"Yes, I think I can relate to her feelings, Michael," I said. "I think I can connect with Dionysus' feelings as well. They showed remarkable restraint beside the stream, but it could be a long night of anticipation!"

"Exactly," replied Michael. "This buildup of expectations is part of the process. Were it not, then surely Dionysus would not have had the incentive to curtail his initiative.

"At the dinner table that night, Arcas, Melissa and Euterpe observed Dionysus and Cassandra more carefully than usual. They were looking for telltale signs to verify the level of attraction which they all knew existed between the two. The couple played it cool. They had purposely agreed to camouflage their feelings as much as possible in order to keep the family guessing. It was an interesting and fun game. It is not so easy to hide something as obvious as love from someone so close and so intuitive. Dionysus and Cassandra played the game so well that they had everyone inwardly guessing.

"It took a long time for both Cassandra and Dionysus to get to sleep that night. They were each trying to imagine what the cosmic sexual experience would be like. They were also freely indulging in fantasy created by their thoughts of just being together.

"They continued to play their game of coolness at the breakfast table. It was a bit more difficult than the night before, for they were both anxious to share their thoughts and feelings. Nevertheless, they did manage to control themselves until they were in the hovercraft on the way to the fields. Then they exchanged their fantasies of the night before and shared their expectations of what was to come. Cassandra was ready to head directly for their love nest beside the stream. So was Dionysus, but he reminded her that a full stomach was not a good time to experiment with cosmic sex. He told her that the high level of energies generated by this type of union would interrupt the digestive process and circumvent the very results they hoped to attain.

"They dutifully went about their tour while their digestion took place. In spite of their longing it was a very pleasant task because they truly enjoyed living and growing things. More than most, they had a sincere love and appreciation of the plant and animal kingdoms. Still, when they first began to feel the pangs of hunger, they knew that the digestive process was completed and the true excitement of the day was about to begin.

"While heading toward their spot beside the stream, their level of expectancy made them giddy with excitement. As Cassandra spread the blanket, Dionysus reassured her that they would not be disturbed. By this time, the energy patterns of their respective auras were being felt very strongly. The interaction of their complimentary electromagnetic force fields was making them almost numb with pleasure vibrations. They very naturally entered into their lovemaking.

"Dionysus had already told Cassandra that it was important to engage in as little conversation as possible.

He had told her that the mind and emotions should be focused on one's own God Center and the God Center of one's mate. Their loveplay quietly progressed from the usual kissing and fondling to the casual shedding of garments. As their beautiful skin tones were unveiled and blended into the splendor of their surroundings, their bodies blended into that oneness that catapults two lovers into ecstasy.

"It would have been very easy for both of them to experience an almost instant orgasm. To have done so would have spoiled their chance of success and would have left them feeling frustrated and unfulfilled. Again, Dionysus had explained to Cassandra the nuclear dynamics involved in cosmic sex. They had a clear understanding about the atomic nature of things in those days. He had told her that it was necessary to excite each other to the point of orgasm, and then to control oneself to prevent the orgasm from occurring. He had explained that each time one reaches that point of orgasm, it causes a tremendous speedup of the electrons whirling around the nucleus of each atom in the body. If the orgasm is contained, then the electron speed continues to build as each successive point of orgasm is reached and held. The longer this process is continued, the more difficult it is to prevent the orgasm once the peak is reached. However, if you can hold off the orgasm for half an hour while reaching and holding a series of peaks, it will then become possible to experience the cosmic sex action-reaction. After about twenty five minutes, it will become very difficult to prevent the peak from erupting into an orgasm. Assuming that you do successfully withhold the orgasm after a sufficient rate of electron speed is reached, then you may possibly enter into the cosmic blanket. This is evidenced by a noticeably intense buildup of bodily heat which results in profuse perspiration. At this point you must remain perfectly still with your thoughts centered on the Divine. Then you will feel as if you and your mate have totally merged into oneness and are enveloped in a warm blanket of love and protection. It is in this state that the window to the soul may open and you may find yourself revealed to yourself. You may also find yourself in soul to soul communion with your mate. Even without the soul communication, you will know that you have attained an entirely new level of consciousness as well as a far more profound respect for the act of love and the magical balance it can provide to the body, mind, emotions and soul. Such an act of love will fill you with the greatest feeling of peace and joy.

"Dionysus and Cassandra were doing just fine considering that this was the first time that they had joined together. They had been in union for about twenty minutes and had reached simultaneous peaks six times. This had already produced a high state of balance in their emotions and in their physical bodies. Dionysus was becoming more confident. It was a confidence born of a lack of experience. After twenty five minutes Dionysus was once more reaching for that point just short of the pinnacle. He was now on unfamiliar ground and was not very sure of himself. He had been noticing that each time he had reached a peak, it had taken just a little longer than the previous time. This time, it was taking even longer. All at once he felt that surge that begins near the base of the spine. He instantly reacted to control and stave off the orgasm. He could not. He felt for a moment that he could, just as he had the previous ones, but it was like standing in front of an avalanche with outstretched arms expecting to stop the inevitable. When it became apparent to he and Cassandra that they could not hold it back, they entered into the experience with enthusiasm and extracted the full measure of enjoyment that the release provided. Tomorrow was another day.

"Although their first union did not provide them with the cosmic sexual experience they had sought, it did serve to bring their bodies, minds and emotions into a high state of balance and harmony. It produced that glow that no two lovers can hide from even the most casual observer.

"They spent the next hour or so lying quietly beside one another, each absorbed in the blissful thoughts of reliving the experience and totally enjoying each other's presence. As they resumed conversation, they learned that they both were consumed with a quiet exuberance. It was quite difficult for them to verbalize, but perhaps it could best be described as a feeling of complete well-being accompanied by the most pleasurable physical sensations of high energy, strength and self-assurance. At any rate, they decided the best way to spend the rest of the afternoon was to remain in this spot and talk.

"The little game they had been playing at the breakfast table that morning and the previous evening would be impossible to continue now. There was simply no way to conceal such self-evident results as the incandescence produced by their intimacy. Their joy, their energy, their happiness, was so full they could not restrain it from spilling over and infecting everyone around them. They did try, but it was hopeless. Arcas, Melissa and Euterpe were almost as happy as the young couple themselves, for when you truly love someone it makes you happy to see them happy.

"Arcas was his usual animated and witty self. He observed that Dionysus must have been showing Cassandra some new experiments in the field today. This brought two self-conscious blushes to the cheeks of the young couple, but it also brought a round of happy laughter from everyone. In a land of such high consciousness there is never any shame connected with responsible behavior of emotionally mature people sharing intimacy. Arcas asked if they would soon be ready for the technology tour. Dionysus responded that it would take at least two more days to complete their tour of the fields.

"The following day was spent making up for the time lost the previous day. It was also spent making up for the time Dionysus planned to lose tomorrow, for tomorrow he and Cassandra would try once again to reach the laughter of the Gods.

"He introduced Cassandra to many varieties of fruits and vegetables that were unfamiliar to her. She had to have a little sample of each one. Dionysus reminded her not to do any sampling the next morning as it would interfere with their afternoon plans. She laughingly responded that no food but kisses would touch her lips after tomorrow's breakfast.

"The next morning they were in the fields early. They were still glowing from their previous union and from being together much of the time. Normally, the type of union which they had experienced will produce a state of balance which lasts for days or even weeks. This balanced condition would provide an excellent basis for their next coupling.

"It would be interesting to relate more to you about the agriculture and horticulture, Joseph," said Michael,

"But quite frankly we can't go into detail about everything, and the main point here is the personal relationships and how they affect the soul's growth and evolvement."

"I quite understand, Michael," I replied. "Perhaps you can tell me another story sometime about the plants and the flowers and the farm animals. For now, I am content to hear more about this version of the birds and the bees. Please continue."

"I thought you would understand, Joseph," Michael countered. "Noontime found Dionysus and Cassandra back beside the stream almost breathless with anticipation and craving to again experience the bliss produced by their joining. Beyond that, there was a strong confidence in both of their minds that they would achieve their goal.

"The atmosphere bore testimony to the high level of their sexual energy. It was volitile. It was almost crackling with the electro-magnetic tension of their excitement. If they had had a sufficient degree of mental and emotional control, they might well have been able to perform teleki-nesis through the use of this incredible power. But as I have said, they were interested in one thing and one thing only. They wanted to experience the bliss of the extraordi-nary and uncontrollable laughter that accompanies the successful culmination of the cosmic sexual union.

"What had seemed to be an almost automatic coupling during their first union was repeated in a similar manner. The difference was in their higher state of balance and knowledge of each other plus the awesome charge of kinetic energy that encompassed them. They would obvi-ously have more difficulty containing their orgasms this time. This, in spite of the understanding they had already gained from their first union. At this point, their feelings were so intense that Dionysus almost lost his control.

They remained perfectly motionless until he was able to regain his composure.

"Neither of them could quite believe the sensational scope of pleasure they were feeling by just being joined together. The realization of such fulfillment made any other experience seem almost academic. As they gazed fascinated into each others' eyes, their extreme psychic sensitivity manifested itself by transporting both of them into a light trance state. While in this condition, their deep souls communed to their conscious minds to reveal part of their life plan.

"They were told that they were to be mates in this life. They were also told that they each would be allowed to visit the other once each year for the next five years. At that time, when Cassandra was eighteen, they would be married and remain together in Ciudad de Oro. It was then made known to them simultaneously that they would not experience the cosmic orgasm which they were seeking. This was to be reserved for future unions. Dionysus now knew why Cassandra had felt so special to him when they first met. Cassandra now knew that there would never be any conflict concerning her affections for Victor. They both were made aware that Dionysus would be the next ruler of Ciudad de Oro, succeeding Heracles.

"As the light trance lifted, they were still gazing entranced into each others' eyes in complete wonderment. The deep love which they had been exchanging had so affected their environment, that many of the little animals had gathered in the area just to share the vibration. As the young couple noticed their new companions, they could not restrain their laughter. It was not exactly the laughter they had been seeking, but it was rich, spontaneous and very, very happy.

"They were so caught up in the total joy of their love and laughter mingled with their soul experience, that they almost forgot about having an orgasm. Not that that would have been anticlimactic, but it will give you an idea of the fullness of what they were experiencing. When their laughter began to subside, other parts of their bodies began to resume the movements that were to insure a mutual climax. They clung together silently for a long time enjoying the reverie induced by their union and by the revelations they had received.

"At dinner that night they finally shared in conversation what everyone had already ascertained through observation. They further shared the information disclosed to them during their light trance. Arcas then confirmed that it had been given to he and Melissa at the time of Dionysus' conception that he would someday rule Ciudad de Oro. Melissa and Euterpe showed their unrestrained delight at the prospect of the future union of Dionysus and Cassandra. Arcas further reassured them that their future reciprocal visits would be arranged so that each six months, one would visit the other for a period of at least two weeks.

"At the end of the meal, Dionysus informed Arcas that he had completed his indocrination of Cassandra and that they would be ready for Arcas to conduct his tour in the morning. It was then that Melissa informed Cassandra that she also wanted to spend a day or two with her after the technological tour was complete.

CHAPTER 14

"Cassandra had never been so happy as she was at breakfast the next morning. To think of her emptiness at the moment that Victor departed for Arcturus seemed like a remote dream. Yet that emptiness had been only about two short weeks ago. It was a miracle of many blessings.

"Arcas told Dionysus and Cassandra that they would go directly to the communications center. If you will bear in mind that Ciudad de Oro was (and is) a functional intergalactic spacecraft, this will begin to give you some idea of the communications capability necessarily built into the craft. For starters, the in-house linkups with every part of the ship were total. These linkups included various monitoring sensors with the ability to detect fire or rupture or atmospheric changes. They also included two way voice and closed circuit television. All monitors were computer controlled and were self-tested continuously. Such community service facilities as sewage treatment and recycling, water distribution and waste disposal were all completely automated and were likewise monitored and controlled from the communications center.

"Naturally the radio and television broadcast studios were located here as well as the interplanetary and intergalactic communication systems. All of this was part of the immense computer system. Arcas had planned a little surprise for Cassandra to demonstrate the capability and range of their communications devices. He placed her before a viewing screen and proceeded to make adjustments on the control panel until an image began to flicker before her eyes.

"As the image stabilized, Cassandra clearly recognized a being who resembled the Novic people. She looked over at Arcas questioningly and he smilingly nodded back to her that they were now in direct communication with Arcturus. Her heart skipped a beat as she thought about Victor. Would it be possible, she thought, that they were going to speak to Victor or Prime Nova? Arcas then began speaking and stated that all was in readiness for the communication to begin. The image on the screen shifted to reveal Victor, Prime Nova and Nova Eight seated together. Cassandra screamed with excitement. Leaping to her feet, she started jumping up and down, unable to contain her emotional energy. When Victor greeted her, she quieted down but was still speechless for a few moments. When she was finally coherent, she and Victor began briefing each other about their various experiences. Arcas, Dionysus, Prime Nova and Nova Eight also joined in the conversation when they could get a word in. Until that moment, Victor had not known about Ciudad de Oro. He was quite surprised. It was certainly an inspired way to instruct Cassandra in the technological capabilities of their communications systems. Psychologically, it was very constructive to have a renewed contact with Victor after her developing relationship with Dionysus had begun.

"After about half an hour they completed their intergalactic communications visit and said their good-byes. Cassandra then wanted to know how such a communication had been technologically possible. She could not even conceive how far away Arcturus was, but she was familiar with the limitations of the physical speed of light and the physical flow of electrical current. Knowing how long it would take such impulses to travel even to the nearest planet made her question how their conversation with Arcturus could possibly have taken place with no time lapse. She was quite puzzled.

"Arcas told her one of the reasons he had arranged this event was to stimulate her curiosity about such matters. He explained it this way. What appeared to be a simple television communication from one physical world to a far and distant physical world, was in reality a complex technological triumph involving a series of transductions from one dimension to another. It works like this. The picture and sound is first converted by transducers from the physical level manifestation to the mental (astral) vibration. From there it is further transduced to the spiritual vibrational frequency levels. From the spiritual levels it is broadcast by computer directed and actuated spiritual laser beams to the distant planet. The transmission on the spiritual frequency is instantaneous. On the receiving end of the transmission, the process is reversed to the appropriate frequency vibration of the receiving planet. To understand some of the technology of the mental (astral) and spiritual realms is to remove some of the superstition and misinformation that surrounds such realities.

"The reason that the transmission must be of a spiritual frequency in order to be instantaneous is because the entire creation is connected by the spiritual plasma and is thus one unified whole, whereas the physical and mental units are mostly detached from each other but are connected by the spiritual plasma. In reality, it is all a biological process. Once one understands this basic fact about all life forms, it then becomes possible to develop the technology to accommodate these facts. Whether one is talking about an atom, a solar system, a human being, a galaxy, a planet, a cell or a universe, one is talking about a biological life form. For any scientist to truly understand this actuality, is to open the door of infinite possibilities for science.

"Cassandra was duly impressed. She was very bright to begin with. And as I have already told you, she was exceedingly intuitive to the non-physical worlds. She suggested to Arcas that since they were still in the communications center, why not try to communicate with Aristaeus or Latona (her father and mother). Arcas replied that he had been informed that they were not in Poseid at the present time.

"From the communications center they went to the manufacturing and industrial complex. Here Cassandra was shown some of the variety that was compressed into this self-contained world. The utilization of computer controlled robots had been developed into a fine art. There was not a sustained high level of industry here. Manufactured products were made with such quality and durability that demand was limited. Consequently more time was spent in maintenance and in research and development than in the manufacturing process.

"Next they went to the healing complex to complete the tour. Since Poseid already had an exceedingly fine healing center, Cassandra was already familiar with many of the healing techniques utilized here. Her father, Aristaeus, was a member of the board and had acquainted her with the necessity of total health care since she was a little girl. Nevertheless, there were still a few interesting things to see. For example, there was the three phase chemical analyzer. This was an extraordinarily complex chemical-electro-mechanical computer analyzer. The theory of its analytical function was that everyone's body chemistry is as unique as their fingerprints. Each one's chemistry is based upon the interaction of their basic genetic makeup combined with their nutritional habits, their psychological-emotional patterns, their mental level and drive, their deep mind or soul evolvement and their spiritual vibration. The analyzer was able to determine the ideal chemical balance for each individual's unique demands by measuring the various interacting components and predicting the correct chemical synthesis. The secret of the instrument's success was its ability to accurately measure the factors of one's soul evolvement and their spiritual vibration. Arcas confided to Cassandra that the computer in the instrument was linked directly to the giant computer orbiting beyond the planet Pluto, which contained the soul record of everyone in the solar system. Since Cassandra had not previously known of the existence of this immense computer system, Arcas briefly explained it to her.

"It had been a very full and fulfilling day. It was time to go home to dinner. Cassandra thanked Arcas for the very special privileges she had received.

"After dinner that night Euterpe and Cassandra entertained everyone with their unrehearsed singing and music. Inspired new songs emerged from their tongues as their happiness found its joyful expression in beautiful new melodies. Cassandra's lyre and Euterpe's flute joined to capture and complement the sounds produced by the other. Everyone was spellbound by the musical enchantment that filled the home. In two weeks, Cassandra had not worn out her welcome. She had become a loved and treasured member of the family.

"At breakfast, it was Melissa and Cassandra who were doing all of the talking. Today the two of them would do their thing together. Melissa suggested that they might tour around the Earth in a spacecraft while they talked about Reath and sex and Mother God. Cassandra thought that would be just fine. She had lots of questions about all three.

"A plot of dense jungle forest about one hundred and fifty feet square descended into the jungle floor leaving a sufficient opening for their saucer shaped craft to rise through on its journey to the skies. Even at this point, it was clearly evident that there wasn't going to be a lot of sight-seeing this day. Melissa and Cassandra were already so engrossed in conversation that they barely paid attention to their exit from Ciudad de Oro. Cassandra had started things by enquiring about Reath.

"Melissa then began explaining. She had been informed by Cassandra that Victor was on his way to Reath now. Having been to Reath herself she knew just how to explain everything. Essentially, she told Cassandra everything that Diane has already related to you concerning Victor's experiences there. In addition to that, however, she also told Cassandra how closely Reath and Ciudad de Oro work together in helping the Earth. Since one is allowed only one incarnation on Reath, many great souls try to select Ciudad de Oro as their next Earth incarnation. One can hardly blame them for that. It is infinitely preferable to the hardship that is so frequently experienced on the Earth's surface.

"Reath and Ciudad de Oro cooperate very closely. It is not always easy to help man of Earth without interfering. They are never allowed to interfere unless the planet itself is threatened. This cooperation is also actively aided by Prime Nova and his race.

"Cassandra was truly fascinated by this story. If she had not been enjoying herself so tremendously in Ciudad de Oro, she might have felt a slight pang of jealousy. Instead, she was very happy for Victor.

"Thus far, neither Melissa nor Cassandra had noticed much of anything. They might just as well have been in the living room at home. As their conversation turned to sex, it was obvious that the only sights that Cassandra would be seeing would be insights. There are few things that can compete with sex for gaining one's attention."

"It's your story, Michael," I reminded him. "You certainly have my attention."

"I didn't think for a minute, Joseph, that you were concentrating on the insects chirping, the fish splashing or the birds singing," Michael said. Then we all three laughed for awhile before Michael continued.

"Melissa grew very serious at this point as she told Cassandra that any serious discussion of sex must have its roots in a clearer understanding of the nature of the duality of God. Melissa then told her that few beings in any world have any clear concept of God at all. Man is forever trying to limit God by saying what God is, what God can and cannot do, etc. For instance, there are many who insist that God is an impersonal intelligent force or energy, but not an individualized being as well. Melissa found it truly amazing how man, in his finite limitations and arrogance, thinks he can circumscribe the intelligence that conceived and energized it all! There have always been those of great intelligence, she said, who not only deny the existence of a God Being, but who also insist that even if there were, such a being would never speak or communicate in any way with anything so insignificant as a human being. Granted, she said, that it must be an exceedingly rare event for God to speak to anyone, still it has been known to occur. She told Cassandra that she was not referring to prophets 'speaking the word of God'. She said she was referring to the actual voice of God.

"She then told Cassandra that a few human beings in the creation had had that experience and that they had told this story. They had stated that God had spoken to them about a dual nature, a duality. They said that this information had been given to them in a direct way by that feminine polarity of God which identified Herself as 'Lucilau' and as 'Mother God'. This is what Mother God said:

" 'Love utilized properly can do anything. Love misused can imprison you. Love released and realized can free you.

'The world needs to understand the duality that exists between God, and the need for love to formulate that union which is perfect and whole. All life has that need. It is by this principle that male and female, positive and negative is formed. Matter and anti-matter, the union, the coming together, all is formed by the principle of love. And love can do all things. I attest to this, for I lived in the void of loneliness, and I peered and saw the pains of my Counterpart and I was helpless, for I could only create, and neither retrieve nor destroy, but thereby I created and the worlds were born. It was the power of our love that manifested all things. It is the power of this love that raised mankind and humankind from a seed and a thought and a dream. It was the need of this love that spun the worlds in their orbits and flowered life in every realm. It is this same need, desire and choice to be together, my Counterpart and myself, that will bridge the worlds entire and culminate our plan for the growth and fulfillment of all life.'

"Melissa then repeated the first three sentences to Cassandra to emphasize that the understanding of these words is really the key to all of life's relationships. To comprehend and live by these truths is the end and purpose of all life. The basis for every sex urge in every form of life springs from the duality of God. It is God seeking God. It is life seeking to complete and renew itself through union and reunion with its perfect counterpart. First, God created that duality by dividing into the positive-negative, father-mother, male-female polarities. From this separation and duality was born all life. As that life matures in the evolution of its own self-consciousness, this allows the Father-Mother aspects of God to come back together in completion of the Divine Plan.

"No one will ever be totally and perfectly fulfilled until they are consciously reunited with their twin soul counterpart. They may reach a very great level of fulfillment, but that total completion can only come from the conscious reunion with the counterpart. It is this feeling of incompleteness that drives one on and on in their search for the Divine, for God.

"As one slowly evolves in their consciousness, their twin soul counterpart is evolving on a parallel course which is constantly drawing them closer and closer together. As one draws ever closer to their twin soul, they are also drawing closer and closer to God. Their attitude towards God is marked by an increasingly greater and greater love. The greater this love of God becomes, the more one is able to perceive God in every form of life, and in every being.

"Every sexual act and every sexual union should be approached with the reverence one reserves for all truly holy things. For in sex, we are dealing with and experiencing our very own life force and essence. When our sexual experience involves another, we are also dealing with their life essence. This drive to be complete and fulfilled seems to force many people into countless sexual encounters. They are never satisfied or satiated, but this only leads them to further promiscuity. Such persons have not learned to respect the divinity in themselves or in another. They do not realize that it is their search for God, for their own identity and for their counterpart that drives them. They are not utilizing love properly. Love has imprisoned them.

"What is basically missing in such conduct is the security that comes in knowing oneself. The act itself is not wrong. It is simply misused through ignorance.

"Love which seeks to use another or to own and control another is wrong. Love which freely gives and exchanges with another to whom one is drawn for that purpose is right. Love which does not recognize and respect the divinity within another is wrong. Love which relates to and cherishes the divine within another is right.

"When two beings come together to express in love the purity and divinity which has drawn them together, there is virtually nothing which they cannot do. This is the way it is with you and Dionysus, Melissa told Cassandra. She told Cassandra that both she and Dionysus were examples of the proper fulfillment of the natural law of attraction. She told her it was not just a matter of coming together in a physical union which properly fulfills that natural law, but it also involves the total physical, mental, emotional and spiritual approach. One's attitudes, motives, intent and understanding are all involved. Making love is not just an isolated physical act. Whether one realizes it or not, the act of love includes our whole being. We cannot separate one aspect from another.

"Cassandra paid close attention to what Melissa was saying. She had thought that any discussion of sex would be on a more mundane level, as is most frequently the case when two people discuss sex. She had anticipated that perhaps they would end up talking about her relationship with Dionysus on a more personal level. However, this clearly was not Melissa's intent. She trusted both Dionysus and Cassandra to know and to do the right thing. She only wanted to give Cassandra a deeper insight into the heart of life."

"I must admit, Michael," I said, "That I, too, was anticipating a more sensual discourse. I'm not disappointed, mind you, it's just that your past graphic depictions preconditioned me to expect more of the same."

"If any future reader will take seriously what has just been said on the subject, Joseph," replied Michael, "They will find that it will vastly improve their sex life on all levels. This in turn will accelerate their consciousness and promote their general health and well-being. The proper expression of love is the natural way that God has chosen to elevate man to Godhood. There is no other pathway to God. All other paths are but blind alleys that lead nowhere."

CHAPTER 15

"By this time in their discussion," Michael continued, "The craft carrying Melissa and Cassandra was over what is now the Sudan in Northeastern Africa and heading north. They were at an altitude of about one mile cruising at a speed of approximately fifteen hundred miles an hour. Melissa instructed the pilot to maintain this course so as to fly over the great pyramid in what is now Cairo, Egypt. As long as they were this close, Melissa thought it would be quite interesting to show this great structure and explain its multi-purposes to Cassandra."

"You mean to tell me," I asked Michael with surprise, "That the great pyramid at Gizeh was already constructed that long ago?"

"Indeed it was, Joseph," he replied.

"Who built it, and why?" I eagerly asked.

"I'll respond to your question, Joseph, by relating some of Melissa's explanation to Cassandra," Michael said, and continued.

"When Cassandra heard Melissa instruct the pilot, she asked Melissa what the great pyramid was. Melissa then told her that it was the greatest man-made structure in the Earth, excluding the great extraterrestrial crafts like Ciudad de Oro. She told Cassandra that the planning and construction of the pyramid had been a joint project of Atlantis and Ciudad de Oro. However, only a few of the leaders of Poseid at the time knew that Ciudad de Oro existed. Few have ever known. Therefore, the participation by Ciudad de Oro was secret.

"Melissa then told Cassandra that the pyramid was built for a number of purposes. First of all, its location coincided exactly with the intersection of the Earth's greatest underground and atmospheric rivers of current. You will remember, Joseph, when I was describing to you how it is possible to tap in to these rivers of current to obtain energy. This location, combined with this structure was able to produce all of the energy required by man in the Earth at that time. The pyramid structure itself possesses inherent energy-gathering ability. When this natural potential was added to the Earth's greatest biological source of energy, it produced a virtually limitless supply. Through secret technology, this energy was transmitted without wires to Poseid and other Atlantean cities. When the destruction of Atlantis became imminent in subsequent milleniums, the ruler of Ciudad de Oro deactivated the energy potential from the pyramid. Subsequent to that time, vandals and plunderers have completely changed the face of the pyramid by removing the original white marble facing stones and the tiny gold capstone.

"Melissa then explained that the great pyramid was the major portal through which astral beings from other planets entered the Earth prior to incarnating in a physical body. There were other portals, of course, but at that time this was the major one. She further explained to Cassandra how initiates to some of the sacred mysteries were indocrinated in the secret inner chambers. The unique properties of the pyramid provided a perfect classroom for training initiates from both the physical and the mental realms.

"Melissa told Cassandra that since the Earth itself was a living being, this connection of the principle biological physical and astral energy flow allowed the Planet Earth to become more self-conscious. She likened it to a human being learning that life after death exists in other (spirit) realms. Once a person becomes aware of their own immortality, it opens the door for limitless growth of their consciousness. The same thing applies to the Earth as a being.

"By this time they had arrived above the pyramid and Melissa instructed the pilot to land. Cassandra was understandably very curious. Her psychic sensitivity was stimulating her to the point where she needed to know and discover more.

"They were met and welcomed by the officials who were responsible for the maintenance and protection of the facility. Melissa was not unknown here. She, herself, was an initiate and a great teacher. On occasion, she had brought candidates for initiation from Ciudad de Oro. With the consent of the Prefect who was responsible for maintaining the inviolability of the initiate centers within the pyramid, Melissa proceeded to enter with Cassandra.

"They proceeded alone and silently along secret passages until Melissa suddenly halted. Cassandra asked what was the matter. Melissa told her that she was about to show her something which very few had ever seen or ever would see. She pledged Cassandra to absolute secrecy. Cassandra of course agreed, whereupon Melissa spoke aloud a word. The intonation of this particular word activated a tone sensitive mechanism which caused a huge stone to open, revealing a large room. They entered the room and Melissa closed the door. Melissa then told Cassandra that this was a special room where extensive records were maintained chronicling man's entire history upon the planet Earth. Someday, Melissa told her, these records would finally be revealed to the public to substantiate man's true history upon the planet. Someday, the records would authenticate many controversial beliefs and would also disprove many others. Many of these records were duplicates of those maintained in Ciudad de Oro.

"It was a fascinated Cassandra who absorbed this information like a sponge. Although they did not have time to see very much, with Melissa's knowledgeable instructions Cassandra learned a lot. Since their journey had taken them a third of the world away from home, it was time for them to return to their spacecraft and begin their journey home.

"The return portion of their outing was spent mostly by Cassandra marveling at the intracacies of life as Melissa continued to teach and demonstrate to her how all life is interrelated and interconnected. So few people in the physical worlds seem to be aware of the connections and communications and cooperation that is constantly unfolding. Melissa assured Cassandra that the gradual dawning of realization of people in the physical worlds was a very vital part of their evolution of consciousness. It is these very discoveries that makes life in the physical dimensions so challenging and so interesting.

"Arcas, Dionysus and Euterpe were all waiting at the spaceport when they returned. It was decided that they would dine out in celebration of the completion of Cassandra's indoctrination. During their meal, Cassandra expressed her sincere and profound appreciation to each one in the family for their unforgettable contribution to her life. The time was approaching in a few more days when Cassandra would be returning to Poseid. Until then, she would spend as much time with Dionysus as possible. They would sleep together until Cassandra left.

"The sadness of Cassandra's departure was softened by the knowledge that Dionysus would be visiting her in six months and she would be returning to Ciudad de Oro in one year. In addition, Euterpe was accompanying her back to Poseid for a visit. The excited young women boarded the spacecraft and in a matter of a few hours they were landing in Poseid.

"They were greeted by Aristaeus, Latona, Apollo and Artemis. Euterpe's excitement matched that of Cassandra when Cassandra had first arrived in Ciudad de Oro. It's one thing to visit an almost ideal world when you come from one less than ideal. It's another thing to leave an ideal world and venture into a more unpredictable environment. By comparison to the Earth today, Poseid was considerably more ideal. By comparison to Ciudad de Oro it was considerably less. Still, human nature always seems to find something fascinating in the flirtation with danger, temptation and risk-taking. Some of the tales that Euterpe had heard about the outside world stirred her curiosity to see and experience those things which were nonexistent in Ciudad de Oro.

"Euterpe's introduction to and indocrination to the ways of Poseid in many ways paralleled the experience of Cassandra in Ciudad de Oro. I will not recount those experiences because it is not crucial or pertinent to our story. Euterpe was lovingly accepted into Cassandra's family and by Cassandra's circle of friends. No one was told of Euterpe's true origin. People were simply told that she was from a certain city in South America, and that their families were friends. Cassandra and Euterpe became the best of friends and confidantes.

"The next five years passed rapidly and slowly for Cassandra. When she was with Dionysus, it was fleeting. These were the years when a great lustre was added to the beauty and wholesomeness of Cassandra. Her talents and abilities were maturing. Although she had become very sophisticated, it was not at the expense of her humility or naturalness. At the age of eighteen, she had attained a surprising level of maturity. Her next reunion with Dionysus would take place in a few months in Poseid. At that time, they would be married and then she would return to Ciudad de Oro to live. In the meantime, Euterpe was staying with her in Poseid to help her with wedding preparations."

CHAPTER 16

"During this time span of five years, Victor was receiving a crash course in intergalactic realities. From the beginning of his journey, he had been amazed at the profuseness of human life throughout the many galaxies. Prime Nova had taken great pains to show him how life in the Earth affects all other worlds. He wanted to emphasize to Victor that Earth was the prototype and the template for mankind to follow in their unfoldment in the physical realms. While it was true that there were many, many physical worlds without the history of strife which was connected with the Earth, it was also true that those strifefree worlds were not forcing the growth of man through the lessons of good and evil. Prime Nova showed Victor that it was actually the pain of learning to rise above good and evil that was the final lesson to be learned by man on his pathway to Godhood. Mastery of this lesson imbues man with the absolute knowledge that love is the only reason to live at all. As the future ruler of Atlantis, it was essential for Victor to have this awareness.

"Victor was now returning to Earth. He would be back in time for Cassandra's wedding. Through his periodic communications with Cassandra while she was visiting

Ciudad de Oro, he had learned of her relationship with Dionysus and he was very happy for her.

"The wedding was a most important event in the Earth. There had been very few times in Earth's history when there had been a marriage link between Ciudad de Oro and the outer world. Although it was not common knowledge that Dionysus was from the underground city, it was known to a select handful. Cronus, Victor's father and present ruler of Atlantis and his wife Rhea, Aristaeus and Latona, Cassandra's father and mother, and Cassandra's most special friends Victor, Aeneas and Iris, were the only ones who shared the secret. Since Aristaeus was such a prominent citizen in the Earth, it was necessary to fabricate an above Earth identity and background for the family of the groom. In a city the size of Poseid, that was not impossible to accomplish. Cronus, as the head of government, arranged for the necessary credentials and background to be input into the proper computer records. Also, a suitable home was selected which would not arouse the suspicion of neighbors. Anyone investigating the background of the groom would only discover that his parents were highly respected, but not widely known space researchers and communicators from South America. This would conveniently account for their frequent long absences. It would be made known that Dionysus worked with his father, Arcas, and that he and his new bride would also be away much of the time.

"It was difficult to tell who was most excited at Victor's return to the Earth, Cassandra or Euterpe. Cassandra's love for Dionysus did not diminish her love or respect for Victor. It had merely changed expression to become a different kind of love. As for Euterpe, Cassandra had told her so much about Victor over the years that she felt as if she already knew him well. She had communicated with Victor a few times from Ciudad de Oro, when he and Cassandra were visiting over the intergalactic communicator.

"Within an hour after Victor stepped from the shuttle-craft that brought him to the Earth from Prime Nova's gigantic spaceship, Okressa, it was obvious to an observer that there was going to be a close relationship between Victor and Euterpe. Euterpe had too many of the qualities of Cassandra to go unnoticed by Victor. Although they did not look alike, Euterpe possessed the same type of radiant beauty and noble bearing. She also had many of the other attributes and talents that made Cassandra so special. As sensitive and as psychic as Cassandra was, she had suspected that Victor would be immediately attracted to Euterpe. It was for this reason that she had brought Euterpe along to help greet Victor at his return.

"The preparations for Cassandra's wedding proceeded happily. Euterpe assisted Cassandra less and less as Victor sought her company more and more. Cassandra didn't mind. She had plenty of help. If there were two people in the universe that Cassandra wanted to see happy and fulfilled, it was Victor and Euterpe. By the time Cassandra's wedding day arrived, Victor and Euterpe confided to her that they were deeply in love and planning their own wedding. Cassandra was overjoyed.

"The Earth has never seen a more beautiful couple than Dionysus and Cassandra. The bride and groom, their parents, brothers and sisters, and many of the guests were all extensions or soul fragments of the Eternals that Diane told you about near the beginning of our story. If you will recall, the Eternals themselves are the major extensions of the Father-Mother God. So, in reality the extensions of the Eternals are themselves Gods. It is true that they are less than the whole, but it is equally true that they are nonetheless Gods. Not all of the Gods and Goddesses of mythology are based on fact, as you know. Few of the tales of mythology bear close resemblence to the actual facts of the lives they are supposed to portray. The same truth applies to all historical persons and events. Most of the history of Earth has been tainted to serve the ends of greed and power.

"Nevertheless, among the great souls gathered at the wedding of Cassandra and Dionysus were some of those beings who would be labeled Gods by future civilizations. The label would be a correct one. They were Gods. It would be equally correct to label all men Gods, for all men have the potential to become one. It is all a matter of degree. Some men can live a hundred lives and never progress beyond the crude state. Others can rise to the heights of beauty and achievement in a relatively few lifetimes.

"Following their wedding, Cassandra and Dionysus left for a leisurely tour of the Earth before returning to Ciudad de Oro. For the next ten years, they would split their time between Ciudad de Oro and Poseid.

"Arcas, Melissa and Euterpe remained in Poseid for a month as guests of Cronus and Rhea. During this time Victor and Euterpe were inseparable. Together, the two families finalized the wedding plans for Victor and Euterpe. Their wedding would take place in Ciudad de Oro, but the young couple would return to Poseid to live. Since Cronus was the ruler of Atlantis, the family of the bride would be subject to the same scrutiny they were exposed to at Cassandra's wedding. People would be more than curious about a previously unknown family that had produced both a son and a daughter linking them to two of the most prominent and powerful families in Poseid. Great care would be taken to maintain the secrecy of Ciudad de Oro.

"The nuptial preparations were elaborate. There had never been a precedent in the Earth or in the physical worlds of such importance wherein Ciudad de Oro was finally linked in such a tangible way to mankind on the Earth's surface. You must bear in mind that Earth is the key world in the physical universe. What mankind accomplishes in the Earth affects all worlds. Therefore the guest list to this wedding reflected the importance of the occasion. It had to include those leaders of the physical worlds whose consciousness made them most aware of the significance of Earth's evolutionary progress. Among the notables attending were Nestor, the ruler of Planet Reath and his wife Berenice and daughter Protogenia, Prime Nova, ruler of the three planet system of Arcturus and of the countless worlds controlled and administered by the Novic people, Ares, ruler of Mars and his wife Aphrodite, to name just a few.

"Those of sufficient consciousness to understand the ramifications of these two marriages linking Ciudad de Oro and Atlantis were somewhat apprehensive. They knew that Earth was the ultimate testing ground in the spiritual evolution and growth of physical man. They knew that Earth was the focal point for the confrontation between good and evil in this evolutionary growth. They therefore knew that this merger would not go unchallenged by the forces of evil. The fact that mankind in Atlantis had reached sufficient awareness to permit such a union would put the forces of evil on notice that they were losing the struggle for men's souls. The threat to evil was clear. If mankind on the Earth's surface were allowed to evolve to the level of Ciudad de Oro, then the forces of evil throughout the universe would be automatically overcome!

"Those who are evil are not stupid. They are not naive. They are not unprepared to defend their territory. Evil has always considered Earth their's. Evil fiercely defends any threats against what it presumes is its territorial prerogative. As the saying goes, the battle lines were being drawn. At stake, men's souls throughout the universe. Atlantis would either reach its potential and change the worlds, or evil would once again triumph and Atlantis would become just another lost civilization.

"The challenge was clear to Heracles, ruler of Ciudad de Oro and Cronus, ruler of Atlantis. These two great beings were perhaps the most spiritually aware leaders in the planet Earth. Both were already cognizant that Dionysus and Victor were to succeed them in their respective leadership roles. It would be incumbent upon them to train their successors most carefully.

"Nestor, who was ruler of Reath, and Prime Nova, leader of countless worlds, were certain that the opposition by evil would manifest itself very soon. From the point of view of longevity, Prime Nova knew better than anyone the danger of the situation. Prime Nova was over fifty thousand years old and had seen similar situations in other worlds many times. The Divine Light that great souls increasingly emit as they evolve spiritually, attracts the forces of evil like moths are attracted to the flame. The lights of a dozen great souls, extensions of Gods, were beginning to burn very brightly in the Earth.

"Mythology in the Earth frequently portrays the Gods and Goddesses as being very capricious. They are often pictured as selfish, unjust, deceitful and disloyal. They are shown to possess all of the frailties of humans along with their powers as Gods. This is true. As the Eternals rise up, one by one, on their return journey to completed Godhood, they have all been guilty in their human expressions of many mistakes. However, the attainment of true Godhood is failsafe. That is where evil comes in. Evil exists to test man every step of the way. Man may sometimes fool man with his hypocrisy, but evil is not tricked because evil induced the hypocrisy to begin with. It is for certain that God is not duped. God is not mocked. None will attain Godhood by cheating in class, by cramming, by cutting classes or by any other ruse or shortcut. Evil will see to that. You will have to have earned your Godhood to be able to rise above both good and evil to attain your rightful place at the table in Paradise beside your true Father and Mother!

"What I speak of is beyond Heaven and Earth, beyond the angels and the saints, beyond the hierarchy and the brotherhood of light. It is beyond prophecy and the limitations of prophecy. It is beyond the Great Blue Wall that separates the one and only true Paradise from all other worlds and illusions. It is the true homeland of the Gods. It is mankind's true home when he leaves behind all of his false gods!

"This, then, was the true meaning of the weddings of Cassandra and Dionysus, of Victor and Euterpe. Their unions signaled the beginning of all-out conflict in the Earth between the powers of good and evil. If good were able to triumph, then Atlantis would mark the turning point in the history of man. If evil won, then Atlantis would begin that painful decline which marks the end of every great civilization that fails to live up to its potential.

"Well, you obviously know the outcome of this particular struggle, Joseph. Since Atlantis is only a controversial memory insofar as man in the Earth is concerned, it is self-evident that evil once again won the battle. But to the credit of our two young couples, they were not responsible for the failure of man of Earth. The seeds of failure were sown during their reigns as rulers of Atlantis and Ciudad de Oro, but it was not of their doing. The treachery of others in high places set into motion a gradual corruption in Atlantis which actually took a few thousand years to fully manifest.

"Diane and I are not going into any further detail concerning the remainder of these particular Atlantean lives of Cassandra and Victor. The main aspects that we wanted to depict consisted of the formation of their characters, their sexual orientation, the continued development of their masculine and feminine qualities and the beginning of Atlantis' decay.

"I think Diane wants to speak at this point."

CHAPTER 17

"Yes. Thank you, Michael," Diane said as she continued her story.

"I just wanted to first mention a few things concerning Victor's preparation while he was on his space journey. After he returned to Arcturus from the Planet Reath, he was assigned by Prime Nova as an officer trainee aboard a huge warship. This particular ship was the command ship of the Western Quadrant of the space sectors controlled by the Novic peoples. Prime Nova considered this to be the safest area, yet one which would provide great diversity of experience for Victor.

"The five years that Victor was away was equal to perhaps fifty Earth years from the point of view of variety of experience, time lapse equivalents and intellectual growth. Some of the worlds he visited were in different dimensions. It was a very wise and mature 'young' man who returned to Earth. He was young in age only. The wealth of his experiences, coupled with his inborn wisdom and intelligence, had prepared him well for his future role as ruler of Atlantis.

"One thing which Michael has not described to you in Ciudad de Oro is the magnificent Hall of the Ancients. This is an incredibly beautiful structure which is used only for public gatherings of the greatest importance and significance. It has an auditorium in the round where performances or ceremonies take place in the middle of the audience. The interior of the auditorium is all gold and soft white with the soft white dominating and the gold accenting. There are many arches through which to enter the auditorium. The architecture of the arches varies from round to ogee, from horseshoe to trefoil, from lancet to Tudor, representing all art forms and cultures in the Earth. Placed strategically around the walls are special prisms. Through these prisms is beamed lights which produce soft rainbows of color the length of the walls to the base of the domes which cap the high ceiling. The interior of the domes is indirectly lighted to provide sufficient illumination for any occasion. The intensity of the dome light emission is infinitely variable. The effect of the gold and white with rainbow hues artistically sprayed upon it is breathtaking, exhilarating and uplifting, yet hypnotic and calming.

"This was the awe-inspiring site of the wedding of Victor and Euterpe. Gathered here for the occasion were the most notable citizens of Ciudad de Oro, along with the others Michael has mentioned from elsewhere. Adding immeasurably to the splendor produced merely by being in such a setting, was an unprecedented event which took place as the wedding ceremony was about to begin.

"The hall had grown quiet. The dome lights had been softened to accentuate the rainbow pastel hues which dominated the walls. The groom was waiting alone in the center of the room as was the custom for this type of wedding ceremony. The radiant bride entered the room unescorted and walked slowly towards her waiting groom. As she entered the room, she was bathed in a very gentle spotlight which followed her until she joined her beloved. At this point, they would normally have been joined by the person officiating the ceremony. In this instance Heracles was to have performed the ritual. Instead, no one appeared. Unbeknownst to everyone except Heracles, a grand surprise was about to occur.

"Suddenly, an intense, brilliant white light engulfed the entire auditorium. Everyone instinctively looked up. As they did, a huge gasp escaped their lips as they beheld a form begin to emerge from the light. As the light descended towards the bride and groom, the form crystallized to become the Great Archangel Michael. Everyone except Heracles was stunned. As the Great Michael stood silently smiling before the young couple, a choir of angels began singing the most beautiful songs ever heard in the Earth.

"All were entranced. No bride could ever hope to experience such an enthralling moment. As the angelic choir lowered their voices to a whisper of song, The Great Michael began to speak quietly, saying:

" 'Beloved Ones. The importance of this union linking Ciudad de Oro to the future ruler of Atlantis has drawn me to your side. The connecting of the idealized society of man in the Earth to the leadership of the outer Earth has been long awaited. It signals once again a great opportunity for mankind in the Earth to advance its spiritual growth to that of Ciudad de Oro and Reath.

'To honor this occasion, I wish to impart to you the correct concept of marriage in the eyes of God. As man grows in his understanding of his true nature, the time comes to leave behind outmoded ideas that chain and limit you.

'Let me speak to you about the institution of marriage.

All who hear these words may relay this to humanity, that the knowledge will be understood forevermore. Now is the time for this knowledge to be relayed to the worlds.

'No man, no priest, no official may marry anyone together with validity in the name of God. No man in the world has this power nor this authority to bind two souls together forever. No man has this right or this power. What is the true meaning of marriage? I will tell you now. It is the coming together of two souls by their own decree, by their own love one for the other, and by their own decisions to live, to produce and to enjoy the company of the next. In the laws of man, to marry means forever. In the laws of God, forever is impractical and has never been the purpose nor the plan.

'We are one—our souls, our identities, our goals. All over the worlds, we are one. We live and exist to learn, to grow, to evolve, to be better, and in the process, to help our neighbor, our friends, our companion entities and souls with us. This union known as marriage is a committment that can be made only by two individuals within their heart. They need no intermediary, no spokesman. In life the coming together is decreed by what is in your heart. Even so, the time when you will leave. This, too, decreed by what is in your heart. No law of man supercedes the law of God's union. The only one who can co-join together two beings is God.

'The only true unity binding marriage is when two individuals in their hearts know that they love one another, know that that love is true and real and unselfishly given— when they, together, enter in prayer to God saying, "Creator God, bless this union in your eyes, knowing that we will learn and live together as long as this may be productive for both, as long as we may live where this is the proper way of our soul—the lessons and learnings that we have—and knowing O God, that when our love, our needs, our ways evolve beyond this union, we leave this union, still in search of Thee."

'The morality of humankind must realize this. The order of life which is to come in the world before you, the union that is binding is the committment that you make one to the other. No law of man is meant to hold you. No decree by a priest or a saint meant to imprison you or stagnate you. But the soul at all times must feel free. And if you are together, it must be by your freedom that you have chosen this path. The laws of man may not supercede free will, for know the truth, whatsoever you sow in deed, you reap. How you live with another will determine how you live with yourself.

'The law of God—all things in the physical world are subject to change. All things in the physical world are temporarily established and laid, even the institution of marriage. It is not against God's law for you to love someone deeply, dearly and sincerely, to live with them, to give all that you have to give, and they to you; and then the day comes when the soul has other needs and yearnings, and the soul must go on. Gaze upon the cycle and wheel of life, the chain of life and reincarnation and incarnation everlasting. It is very rare for two souls to establish the rapport and the journey to travel through life forever together. When it does happen, it is the most beautiful of all things. But understand, that union is by their free will, and at no time do they feel imprisoned, at no time do they feel as if they are trapped, encased or lost. The main key to marriage is free will, freedom. And if your love is real, you will understand always the needs of your partner, the needs of your mate. And at times these needs may be different than your own. And when the day comes that when your growing and the growing of your mate depends upon your honestly facing this situation and growing even further, and if that growing means that you must leave one another, then know that the growing, the freedom, the love as placed by truth will show you the way.

'So many individuals live a lifetime in frustration, pain and anguish, fear and doubt—when their own love, one for the other has changed, that they do not face the reality that total love is also total honesty, is also understanding the needs of another. Perhaps the whole of the world is not ready for this concept just yet.

'This attitude that I speak of does not mean promiscuity, does not mean that an individual may move from one life, one mate to the next without remembering the law that what you do to another inevitably will return to you. As such, this principle of a love far reaching, of Divine Love, this is where we are leading—a love that is unselfish to the needs of your mate, a love that would adhere to the growth of your mate even beyond your own needs if such was meant to be. It is a love that will accept sacrifice if sacrifice means someone you love will be better and happier. It is a love that is not possessive, nor jealous— a love that would not demand stagnation on the part of one mate to the next.

'Understand me. The only value of a marriage that can ever exist is the vow that two beings make to one another before their God. The only validity of this marriage is within their own souls and before that God Who is all.'

"The emotion and the feeling of love that pervaded

the auditorium as the Great Michael spoke was awesome. The angelic choir had continued their whisper of song all the while that the Great Michael spoke. They also played a typical game that happy angels play at such a joyful occasion. They would blend themselves individually into the little rainbows cast by the prisms onto the walls. Then the rainbows would seem to be dancing on the walls as the angels moved in and out of them. All were spellbound and totally captivated by the occasion and all that it portended.

"The Great Michael then congratulated Victor and Euterpe. He spoke to them quietly and then embraced each of them warmly and affectionately. As he was embracing them, an angel simultaneously appeared to, and embraced, every single person in the audience. No one in attendance would ever forget this night.

"This concludes our description and reference to the Atlantean lifetimes of Cassandra and Hector. As we have indicated before, it is not our purpose to go into great detail concerning any one lifetime. It is rather our intent to describe those important incarnations and portions of lifetimes that best accentuate the cumulative effect of a soul's physical evolution on the pathway to enlightenment and Godhood.

"Before we continue, Joseph, an unexpected event has just taken place. The Archangel Gabriel has just appeared here to us and asked permission to interject some information which he hopes for you to include in your book. He asks for permission to speak to you now," Diane exclaimed.

"Just before you said that, Diane," I replied, "I felt a great rush of energy accompanied by a feeling of euphoria.

Quite obviously, it's the Archangel Gabriel's presence that I feel. I will be highly honored to have him speak to me."

"Thank you, Joseph," Gabriel said as he began communicating to me on a telepathic level.

"As you perhaps suspect, it is not often that I come to speak to those on the physical dimensions. On most occasions when I do, it is because the Father sends me. Such is now the case.

"The book that you have been asked to write by Diane and Michael has been divinely ordained. Although it is a simple story of the journey of two souls through a series of physical incarnations in the Earth, it has a parallel in the lives of countless other souls now alive in the Earth. There are millions who can be comforted and aided by the information which has already been given to you.

"The principle thing that I wish to speak to you about is this; the situation in the Earth today is identical to that in the time of Atlantis when Victor and Euterpe were married. The spiritual light of a number of individuals is burning very brightly. Earth once again has the opportunity to rise to its true potential.

"Remember what Michael and Diane have told you. When the spiritual consciousness of man becomes too high, the threat to the forces of evil compels them to respond with vigor. Just as in Atlantis, the soul of man is at stake throughout the universe. Evil will not back down. It cannot and will not. Man in the Earth is the center and the focal point of this struggle. Unlike Atlantis, this is mankind's final opportunity to rise above both good and evil and enter Paradise with the Father and the Mother.

"You have noticed the explosion of the acts of violence,

evil, greed, corruption, malevolence, ill will, suffering, malice and cruelty that has erupted with increasing frequency and severity in the Earth. Many of these self-same acts of depravity have been perpetrated in the name of God and good. That is why man must rise above both 'good' and evil. In truth, good cannot oppose evil. The reason it cannot is that in the act of opposing, it becomes like unto that which it opposes. By its very nature, evil can use any means to oppose good. By its very nature, good cannot oppose evil without being transformed in the process to that which it opposes. It is impossible for good to commit the identical acts which it opposes in evil and remain good. For good to use the excuse and the alibi that its evil acts are committed in the name of God, does not transmute the evil acts. These are the games of hypocrites, liars, self-deceivers and fools!

"You may logically ask what to do. If good cannot fight evil, how can victory be achieved in this struggle? The answer is obvious. Evil will destroy itself. Do you think for a moment that the Father and the Mother would send mankind on this long journey and quest, and abandon him now? Never! In the plan of the Father and the Mother, Evil's own greed and excesses will pit it against itself. In the final analysis, evil will consume evil. Mankind is not helpless.

"The challenge now is for man to really learn what it means to go within himself. The most exciting thing about self-discovery is that it produces a revelation and an understanding of all life. True self-discovery brings about the realization of the unity and similarity of all living beings. It is only a matter of degree that separates us in the manifestation of the same characteristics that are inherent in us one and all. We each have good in us. We each have evil in us. We each have the need to experience the effects of good and evil in our lives. And finally, we each have the opportunity to rise above both good and evil and assume our rightful destiny beside the Father and the Mother in Paradise.

"This is all I have to say at this time, Joseph," the Archangel Gabriel said, then concluded, "To all who read your book will come the Angels of Love and of Light. Those who are truly seeking to rise above good and evil will have the help they seek. This is a direct promise from the Father and the Mother. Their promises are kept. I thank you."

"Thank you, Beloved Gabriel," I replied. I was too surprised to say anything else.

"Gabriel's remarks need no further clarification from Michael or me," Diane said. "Although we did not know that he was coming to speak, what he said beautifully augments our portrayal of the spiritual struggle for men's souls that took place in Atlantis and is taking place now.

CHAPTER 18

"Back in the realm of spirit, Cassandra and Hector viewed their lives as Cassandra and Victor with a great measure of satisfaction. It had been a richly rewarding experience in every possible way. They had tasted all of the fruits of the vine that Earth has to offer and they had not been corrupted in the process. They had come close a few times," Michael stated, and continued, "but they remained faithful to the promise and expectation of this most fulfilling of all of their Earth lives.

"Once again Cassandra and Hector consulted with the wise ones who maintain the records and projections of events in the physical Earth. It saddened them to learn of the projected demise of the great civilization which they had helped create. It was estimated that it would take at least several thousand years for evil to totally corrupt the fruits of thirty milliniums. But the signs seen from this dimension were unmistakable. Many in high places were already infected. Many were already doing the work of evil without even realizing it. Evil is so insidious.

"It was an easy decision for Cassandra and Hector to decide against any further incarnations during this time span in the Earth. They turned their attention towards helping prepare others who were planning to incarnate.

"The actual downfall of Atlantis was triggered by a denial of God. Most people who are aware of the past existence of Atlantis think that its fall came about solely because evil triumphed over good. Evil did triumph, but not for generally understood or accepted reasons. It is not possible for evil to win if mankind accepts God. It is not possible for mankind to accept both God and evil. In order to accept God, one has to learn to listen and heed that still small voice within their very own being. You cannot accept God as long as you believe that anyone else has a greater authority or connection with God than you. You cannot accept God if you fear retaliation for following God's true voice within you. One must come to realize that evil's basic weapons and tools against mankind consist of threats, intimidation and psychological warfare.

"Probably the only true mortal sin is for man to deny the actual prompting of his own God nature from within his own conscience.

"The final collapse of Atlantis came about through the denial of God by one who was in power at that time. Instead of following his own inner promptings, which were correct, he yielded through fear to the intimidation of one representing the ultimate evil. It's as simple as that.

"It was not pleasant for Cassandra and Hector to observe helplessly from another dimension. However, there was nothing they could do about it. Since both of them were still required to go through future incarnations, they began making plans. They learned that mankind had one more opportunity to reach his potential in the Earth. It would require a cycle of approximately twenty six thousand years to fulfill. They would do their share!

"In the next fifteen thousand years Cassandra and Hector incarnated fifteen times each. By agreement they did not incarnate at the same time. One or the other always remained behind to assist in every possible way from the land of spirit.

"The high level of their past attainments in the Earth allowed them to experience a number of important roles. The shattering of Atlantis had left only remnants of that great civilization scattered around the planet, but they were important remnants. When the extent of the probable disintegration of Atlantis was realized, some of the resourceful leaders had begun efforts to decentralize, which had resulted in strong cultural influences being implanted in Central and South America, Northern Africa, the Middle and Far East, New Zealand and Easter Island. These were the areas upon which Cassandra and Hector concentrated. Hector was attracted more toward the Orient and Cassandra more toward Central and South America.

"These various cultures formed the building blocks upon which the new great civilization would be based. The final episode of the conflict between good and evil in the Earth would see a worldwide civilization consisting of all the great souls since the beginning of time engaged in a titanic struggle to decide the fate of mankind.

"As the zodiacal clock moved closer to the next great confrontation between good and evil, Cassandra and Hector associated themselves more and more with that large band of enlightened souls who are sometimes referred to as the White Brotherhood. This found them concentrating on the spiritual centers of influence in the Americas, in Northern Africa and the Middle East and in the Himalayas. This finally brought them to the series of incarnations which culminated in Troy in the twelfth century B.C.

"After ninety nine lifetimes in a physical body in the Earth, Cassandra had experienced just about everything a woman could ever want or imagine. She really had no need or desire for further incarnations at this time. Although she had not yet reached that ultimate level of attainment in the physical world wherein the soul returns directly to God, she knew that that experience was not possible or in sequence for at least another several thousand years. It therefore took some persuasion from the Brotherhood of the Light to convince her that she should incarnate in Troy along with Hector and many others who planned to work together. She finally condescended and decided to become the daughter of King Priam through one of his concubines named Jacinda.

"Jacinda had been Iris. Iris, you will recall, had been a sister to both Cassandra and Hector in prior lives and had also been one of Cassandra's best friends in her major Atlantean incarnation. The usual careful plans were made. Jacinda wanted to bear one of the king's children and she dearly wanted it to be a little girl. Cassandra arrived three years after Hector was born.

"Hector had chosen the queen herself as his mother. Hecuba had been Hector's (Victor's) mother, Hilda, in his first Atlantean incarnation.

"As mythology accurately recalls in this instance, no woman in Troy was more beautiful than Cassandra—no man more brave or handsome than Hector.

"The Brotherhood of the Light was seeking to form a practical alliance between the Trojans and the Greeks as a basis for the next great super civilization. The plan was to have a large number of the brotherhood incarnate in both Greece and Troy. It was reasoned that with so many great spiritual beings working on both sides for the same thing, success would be virtually assured. The actual outcome of the experiment only confirms the naivete that spirit has frequently been guilty of demonstrating in the past with regard to the realities of the physical worlds. It has invariably been found to be true that great beings have great egos. In the physical worlds, the ego has always been one of the easiest things for the forces of evil to manipulate. In the mental and spiritual worlds, the ego is more subtle.

With so many truly great souls incarnated at one time, it must have been very amusing for evil to play their egos, one against the other. Just think of the scenario. Here we have the Eternals, represented in mythology by the Titans, the Olympians and others. In the physical Earth, these Gods were represented in their human forms. These human forms possessed awesome powers and abilities, and because they were often treated as Gods they tended to act like they thought Gods were supposed to act. The forces of evil encouraged the philosophy, 'You are a God. Right or wrong you are still a God, therefore you can do whatever you want to do'. The alliance that was supposed to have been formed was to have been based upon the highest spiritual principles. High spiritual principles could hardly be expressed in such an egotistical environment. There were simply too many Gods, each one wanting to be the most important God. Without the attribute of Divine Love to help them to see, accept and understand the God nature in each other, they were easy prey to evil.

"This, unfortunately, was the environment in which Cassandra and Hector grew up. It was a miracle of sorts that both of them were untouched by this ego madness. Their careful preparation before incarnating, their high evolvement in physical life experience, their sensitivity to divine aid and their extensive help from both worlds enabled them to grow in wisdom and in love.

"The reputation which mythology has bestowed upon Cassandra of Troy is basically false. It is true that she was the most beautiful of King Priam's daughters. She was the most beautiful woman of Troy. Her extraordinary beauty in itself was responsible for many of the false tales which jealous women and frustrated suitors spread against her. In her case, her beauty had been earned by many lifetimes of dedication and achievement. It was wasted on Troy.

"Insofar as the mythological account of Cassandra's experience with Apollo, I would now like to set that straight. Mythology states that Cassandra agreed to make love to Apollo in exchange for Apollo granting to her the gift of prophecy. Mythology then states that after Cassandra received the gift of prophecy from Apollo, she refused his advances, whereupon he moistened her lips with his tongue and ordained that no one would ever believe her prophecies.

"What really happened was that Cassandra was born with the gift of prophecy. She had no need of Apollo or anyone else granting her any psychic gifts. She was an extension, or soul fragment, of one of the Eternals, and was just as much a God as Apollo. Furthermore, Apollo was part of the same Eternal as Cassandra. They had been brother and sister when Cassandra had her great Atlantean incarnation and they had a very deep and natural love for one another. In the Troy incarnation, Cassandra and Apollo had become lovers when Cassandra was sixteen and they remained lovers until Apollo left Troy some seven years later.

"Rather than spurning Apollo, Cassandra achieved with him as a lover what she had never achieved with Victor or Dionysus or any other. Their sexual compatibility made them intensely loyal to each other. Neither of them ever gave a thought to taking another mate while they had each other. It was with Apollo that Cassandra finally experienced the full transcendence of cosmic sex.

"They had been lovers for perhaps two years when it began to surface. Their unions, though never casual, began to grow ever more soul stirring and powerful. The greater the intensity became, the more each responded on a higher level of consciousness. It was as if each time they made love, they peeled away another layer from their souls. Each time a layer was peeled away, more previously learned knowledge became exposed. As more knowledge lay exposed, this led in turn to a continuing display of increasingly higher consciousness. If they were able to remain together, it seemed inevitable that they would eventually reach that pinnacle that most lovers are not even aware exists. At the time, they themselves were not actually aware of what it was they were subconsciously striving towards.

"The initial infatuation that caused them to become lovers rapidly deepened into love. As their relationship progressed, their expanding consciousnesses elevated their love to a very high spiritual level. And then it happened. One day as they were making love, Apollo started giggling uncontrollably just as he entered into his orgasm. This unexpected reaction triggered a similar reaction in Cassandra. The giggling continued intermittently for about fifteen minutes. During this time, each time one of them would giggle it would stimulate that response in the other. They found it to be an intensely satisfying experience.

In comparison to their preceding unions, this one had brought them to a state of balance and exuberance not previously achieved. As they lay beside each other delighting in this new level of sexual bliss, they drifted off into a light sleep. When they awakened, they discovered that they felt unusually refreshed and energized, but at the same time they were possessed by a deep calmness and strength.

"Since they had never experienced the giggling before, they decided to discuss it thoroughly from the point of view of being able to repeat their performance. What was it that they had done differently this time? They concluded that it was the conscious dedication which they had agreed to prior to their actual union. This dedication consisted of each one speaking aloud words to the following affect, 'I ask that my love for God, for you and for myself be reflected in the level of joy and fulfillment that results from our joining together'.

"The preceding two years had already awakened in them the 'instinctive' techniques which they had learned in other lifetimes. Step by step, they had progressed in their lovemaking until they had each reached the level of their great Atlantean incarnation. Now they would reach that plateau where the laughter of the Gods sealed their unions with its own special brand and label of love.

"From that point on, almost every time Cassandra and Apollo made love, the climax was characterized by that uncontrollable laughter which signifies that two human souls are in perfect love harmony. What was first experienced as spontaneous giggles, quickly transcended to become the laughter that can balance all life!

"The only Earthly experience that can truly surpass the uninhibited laughter and joy of the cosmic sexual experience is for one to be linked with their twin soul during the experience. To exceed that, one can only think in terms of a face to face union with God.

"As you have no doubt correctly concluded by now, very little reliance can be place in the historical authenticity of most mythology. However, this is not to say that mythology is not rich in allegory and entertainment, in wisdom and instruction. The lessons of mythology are little different from other historical accountings in their accuracy. History is extravagantly inaccurate. It is frequently written to reflect the views of those with the power. The source documents of most historical writings are of dubious objectivity and accuracy. One has only to think of the example of two or more eyewitnesses reporting the same incident. You will usually hear as many different versions of the incident as you have witnesses. When historical events are being reconstructed entirely from written documents, an objective person cannot place full faith in the views expressed.

"In future times, the near future I may add, mankind in the Earth will have access to completely accurate information systems detailing what has actually occurred in the Earth during the past twenty five thousand years. These systems will be accessible in such a way as to provide color television replay of any incident to have occurred in the Earth since Atlantis.

"You will be interested to know that there is a device on the dark side of the Earth's moon which was constructed by the Eternals during the time of Atlantis. This device has been recording *every* event in the Earth. The man-made planet beyond Pluto, as we have previously told you, is likewise recording every event in the entire solar system. Some day soon, as man of Earth sits in front of his television receiver, he will see a replay of actual historical events and situations. He will be shocked by what he discovers. There are many unbelievable things which are true and many widely held beliefs which are totally false. It will be traumatic for many.

"We do not believe that our accounting to you of the lives of Cassandra and Hector will be traumatic to those who are familiar with the mythological version. However, we do think that our version will be more entertaining and instructive.

"To get back to Cassandra for one last time, let me say this. The love relationship of Cassandra and Apollo produced a degree of cosmic consciousness in each of them which made them very different from others. They found after a time that Hector and Andromache were about the only ones with whom they could relate. The forces of evil were growing so great around them, that they each became victim to increasing acts of deceit and envy. Events forced Apollo to leave Troy. He planned to travel to Macedonia and create a new life. He planned to send for Cassandra as soon as possible. They did not see each other again until they crossed over once more into the land of spirit.

"There is no point in detailing a large number of events in the remainder of Cassandra's life. Some of the things referred to in mythology are true. Some are not. She was a prophet. Since many of her prophecies concerned ominous events to come, she could justifiably be called a prophet of doom. Had her warnings been heeded, perhaps history would have turned out differently. The tragedy of her life was that she was the consummate woman, and that the precious flower of her femininity was squandered upon a corrupt society. Fortunately for her, she had lived the experience of more idyllic lives in the Earth. Aside from that, it must be emphasized that for one to achieve the cosmic sexual experience makes any lifetime worthwhile. So, in spite of all the pain and unpleasantness in the life of Cassandra of Troy, she did finally reach the zenith and the mountaintop which she had sought for a hundred lifetimes."

CHAPTER 19

"Now that Michael has concluded his version of the story of Cassandra, I will fill you in briefly on Hector's lifetime in Troy," said Diane.

"Mythology has treated Hector a bit more kindly than Cassandra. Not that he had an easy life, mind you. Far from it, but at least he emerged a hero. Some of the soul memories that Hector had accumulated in his previous Earth lives rushed forth at an early age to fulfill the promise of this life. We find him as a child in the palace of his father, the king, demonstrating his attributes of valor, justice, intelligence, loyalty and strength. As a teenager, his soul characteristics of wisdom, compassion and forbearance surfaced strongly. Also as a teenager, his powerful sex drive began asserting itself in the various forms available to a prince of the royal household.

"There was not the sexual sophistication of enlightened Atlantean parents to guide him. Although he was a favorite son of the King and Queen, he was left mostly on his own with the palace tutors and courtiers to learn about life. And learn he did. They were cooperative teachers, he was a willing student. He was not in want for female companionship. For one surrounded by such opportunity and temptation, Hector was surprisingly disciplined. While

191

he freely indulged his sexual drive, he did so within the bounds of restraint and need. He did not exploit others. In the process of his sexual growth and learning, he rapidly relearned many of those previously discovered sexual realities emblazoned upon his soul engrams. By the time he met his future wife, Andromache, he was sexually prepared for an enduring and fulfilling relationship. What I mean by this is that he had reached the point of being able to relate to a person on all levels—physical, mental, emotional and spiritual.

"Relating to Andromache in a total way was perhaps the easiest thing Hector ever did. You see, Andromache had been his beloved wife, Euterpe, in Atlantis. Their soul attachment was so deep and pure that their mutual love exploded from the moment they first met. There was never any doubt that they would marry one another.

"With the exception of Cassandra and Apollo, a more devoted couple could not be found in Troy. The difference was that Hector and Andromache were married according to convention, whereas Cassandra and Apollo were lovers only.

"Many of the deeds and exploits which mythology attributes to Hector are true so I will not be repetitive. What history and mythology do not reveal is the private life which we are chronicling here. I did not relate to you the quality of the sexual relationship between Victor and Euterpe in Atlantis. I did go into some detail regarding Victor's affair with Protogenia on the Planet Reath. Let me state now that Euterpe and Victor enjoyed the fullest and most satisfying sexual relationship possible, short of that final pinnacle evidenced by the uncontrollable laughter of the Gods. Like Cassandra, Hector would scale that peak in Troy.

"It wasn't until after their son, Astyanax, was born that Andromache and Hector began to reach the point in their intimacy where the promise of the cosmic sexual experience became possible. Before the arrival of Astyanax, they did not even suspect the heights to which their pure love would lift them. No matter how far a soul has advanced in a previous life, one does not reach the peak instantaneously in a given life. There is always the reawakening process. There is always the purification. There is no mockery on this sacred ground. One's own deepest soul-self will see to that.

"The arrival of little Astyanax brought a new dimension to their love relationship. Soon the intensity of their unions began to unlock the doors to their souls. As they became more centered in their mutual love of God and of each other, the unfolding process quickened. The time had arrived for Hector and Andromache to learn and experience the full meaning of the words, "love is the only reason to live at all!".

"The 'instinctive' relearning process induced by their previously learned knowledge being released from their souls, began to exert its influence upon the atomic structure of their bodies. Each of their unions was now producing a greater and greater acceleration of the electrons whirling around their atomic nuclei. Michael referred to this phenomenon when he was describing the relationship between Cassandra and Dionysus. He did not go into any detail beyond mentioning that after a sufficient rate of electron speed is reached, one may possibly enter into the cosmic blanket. There are many other effects to be gained by a controlled acceleration of the electron speed within the body.

"First of all, the cosmic sex process is nature's way of

natural bodily detoxification. This speeding up of electron movement on the atomic level causes a throwing off by centrifugal motion of toxic waste buildup within the atomic, molecular and cellular structure. The accompanying heat produced by the speedup of electrons burns up the toxic wastes that have been spun off. This is very important. The entire cosmic sex process is dependent upon a bodily purification on the atomic level. You see, it is the atomic level that carries within it the memory spectrum and the access to all frequencies of consciousness. If this level of one's being is clogged by toxins, then it is equivalent to short-circuiting one's cosmic connections. On the other hand, when the body is detoxified, then the pathway to cosmic consciousness becomes open.

"As the speed of the orbiting electrons approaches the speed of light, one's aura becomes more visible, one becomes more vibrant and healthy. Should the speed of light be attained, then one's body would literally glow and one would possess the consciousness to accomplish 'miracles'. This is the very thing that took place during the time of Jesus of Nazareth. However, I am not going to discuss that. That's not a part of this story.

"Andromache and Hector were literally transforming themselves and each other through their enlightened love. They were now learning to control their sexual unions in a manner that would allow the fullest expression of love. They were using their minds and emotions, their souls and spirits, as well as their bodies in relating to each other. They allowed themselves to be completely vulnerable—to be open and natural, to be honest, trusting and intuitive. Hector finally learned to control himself fully so as not to precipitate a premature orgasm. The stage was set. Their human atomic reactor power plants were ready to function in a manner to delight their wildest expectations."

"I like your analogy, Diane," I interjected.

"Thank you, Joseph," she replied, and then continued. "The human being is the most perfect atomic reactor that could ever be invented. In order for it to function properly though, it requires an enlightened male and female to activate the machinery and control the power. In the operation of the human power plant you have a radioactive rod penetrating a critical mass in such a way as to produce a tremendous increase in the speed of the electrons whirling around their nuclei. The atomic composition of the penis and the vagina is such that the friction produces an excitation and an acceleration that radiates throughout the entire body. It affects all levels of the human being including the physical, mental, emotional, spiritual and beyond. Mankind has always wondered just what it is that produces the incomparable thrill of the orgasm. It is a nuclear explosion of sorts involving an induced amalgamation of the spiritual self with the physical, mental and emotional self. This amalgamation is induced by friction. The friction is not only physical but is also electro-chemical-magnetic. It involves the atomic structure on all the various levels as stated, as well as the electro-chemical-magnetic exchange. The orgasm could perhaps be likened to the spark produced by touching wires connected to a positive and negative source. When the friction generated in the genitals accelerates the electrons sufficiently, it draws and attracts the spiritual part of one's being to connect more fully and powerfully until the orgasm is sparked. This cause and effect takes place whether one uses the sexual faculty for a higher purpose or not. However, the quality, the power, the purification, the edification and all other aspects of the orgasmic potential are dependent upon the degree of knowledge and know-how of the lovers. To the extent that lovers can incorporate the cosmic requisites that we are stating in our story, then to that extent can they benefit from the available potentials of their union.

"Andromache and Hector were just reaching the point of extracting the fullness of the promise of their love relationship. The nights of their unions were now marked by the reverberations of uncontrollable laughter that escaped their chamber and echoed through the palace corridors. Everyone noticed the increasing glow radiating from the two lovers. It was too good to last. At least in Troy, for Troy's days were now numbered.

"The increase in consciousness and perceptivity brought about by their cosmic unions enabled Andromache and Hector to realize that they would soon be parted by fate. Andromache knew in her heart that Hector would soon die in battle, but she pleaded with him anyway to refrain from personal combat. Hector knew from deep within that he could not cast aside the skills and valor acquired in a hundred lifetimes to prolong his life span in this life. As dearly as he loved Andromache and Astyanax, his destiny was ordained by the overall events which were already in motion. It was now only a short time before Hector would fall in battle. By any measure, Hector knew that he had achieved his original goal in the physical worlds of attaining consummate manhood. He had enjoyed the total range of experiences that one associates with manhood in the physical body. A hundred lifetimes had then been crowned by reaching the fulfillment of love's promise as released and realized in the 'laughter of the Gods!'."

CHAPTER 20

"Well, Joseph," said Diane, "that is the story of what really happened to Cassandra and Hector as compared to the purely mythological version. The aspects of their lifetimes as Cassandra and Hector which history chooses to emphasize, does not present any idea at all of their true natures or spirituality.

"We are sincerely hopeful that our story presents a plausible basis for understanding the cumulative effect of many lifetimes upon any given lifetime. Cassandra and Hector started out from the world of spirit with the goal of attaining all that a woman or a man could reasonably hope to attain in the Earth at that time. Their goal was to become the consummate woman and the consummate man. It took them one hundred lifetimes. They achieved their goal and their souls advanced accordingly.

"With your permission, we would now like to conclude our story by relating to you what Michael and I have experienced in our last six incarnations. You will see that it is quite a contrast to what Cassandra and Hector had to learn."

"Please continue, Diane," I said.

"Without delving into any background at this point,

Joseph, I will start by telling you of a lifetime I experienced in Rome, Italy in the second century A.D.

"I chose to be the oldest child, a daughter, of a Roman Senator. Many changes were taking place during that time as the influence of Christianity began to alter much of the culture of the Earth. My mother in that life was a beautiful and gentle soul. My father was basically a good man, but he was strongly affected by the mores of the subculture of the then ruling class of the Roman Empire. He tended to be domineering in family relationships. As a very young child, he made it obvious to me that he would have preferred a son as his firstborn. This really did not bother me too much at the time. I loved my father and I felt in my own childish way that I could adapt somewhat to his expectations. Besides, I liked the idea of being a boy. Actually, I identified in the strongest of ways with little boy activities. This pleased my father.

"When I was six years old, my brother was born. At last my father had his son. As my brother grew older and began to walk and talk, my father's attention shifted more and more to him and away from me. My mother tried to give me more attention to compensate. She had noticed that I much preferred to play with little boys and she recognized the need to cultivate more feminine characteristics in me. Since I loved my mother very much I cooperated with her, but this did not change my inner attitude. The simple fact is that I identified much more with boys than with girls. For reasons which I could not understand, I thought of myself as a little boy.

"When I was ten years old, my parents decided to hire a tutor for me. The tutor was a beautiful and brilliant seventeen year old girl named Lucretia. My name was Paphia. I remember the difficulty I had at first in adjusting to the discipline of formal study. Lucretia, though young, was very good. She inspired me by her range of knowledge and her patience. She showed such a love for me that I found it quite easy and natural to love her as a friend as well as my teacher. As our relationship grew in scope and affection, I looked less and less to my parents for guidance and love.

"By the time my menses arrived at the age of twelve, I had begun to lose interest in being around boys. I was definitely and strongly attracted to the games, pastimes and interests of boys and men, but I found new emotions gripping and pulling me. Powerful and mysterious forces were prompting my thoughts and desires in directions not suggested by my tutor. In fact, new sensations of desire and arousal were sweeping over me and causing me to look at Lucretia as someone more than my tutor.

"For her part, Lucretia obviously sensed my increased interest in her and began to restructure my lessons accordingly. It was at this time that I started receiving instructions in bodily and emotional changes associated with puberty. It was at this time that I became more aware of the reproduction process and the cycle of life. The more I learned of these subjects, the greater became the libidinous drive within me. I did not know how to control or direct this drive. I was too self-conscious to question Lucretia about such an intimate dilemma. And yet, I found that Lucretia was the main object of my sexual interest. Since we were both females, this did not seem consistent with the male-female roles she was teaching me. I certainly did not understand why I should have such a strong attraction towards Lucretia and I was too embarrassed to discuss it with her. Eventually, however, my libido became so strong that it made me very bold.

"Up to this point I knew nothing about masturbation. With no outlet or release for my immense pent-up kinetic energies, I decided to follow my instincts. My inner promptings told me that Lucretia would understand. One day as she touched me gently on the arm to make a point, I placed my hand upon hers and held her hand to my arm. As I did so, I looked into her eyes for approval. I tried to communicate as much love with my glance as possible. Without hesitation, she responded by placing her free arm around my shoulder and drawing me to her bosom. She followed this movement by kissing me lightly on the cheek. My heart pounded so wildly with excitement and pleasure and expectation that I could not believe it. With my cheek pressing against her bosom, I could feel her heart also pounding as well as her rapid breathing keeping pace with mine. We remained in this embrace for some time until a feeling of peace and total contentment had replaced the urgent passion that had seized us.

"Our relationship began to change quickly from that point onward. What had been a tutor-student-friend arrangement broadened and blossomed to include becoming cherished companions, confidantes and lovers. Yes, we became lovers. It was the easiest and most natural thing in the world. In retrospect, I am amazed at the restraint that Lucretia had demonstrated in our past relationship. She was a lesbian, and yet not once did she violate the trust of her position until I made the first overt move. Even then, neither of us ever considered for a moment that any trust had been broken.

"For five more years, until I was seventeen, our liaison continued. No one in my family ever suspected the slightest thing. During this time, Lucretia also tutored my brother. She had long since been accepted and treated as a family member herself. Everything seemed almost ideal until the day my father announced to my mother that he had arranged a marriage between me and the son of another powerful senator.

"Lucretia and I were shattered by the news. We were truly and deeply in love. The thought of losing each other was devastating. I pleaded with my mother to intercede in my behalf to persuade father to change his mind. It was hopeless. Many, if not most marriages were arranged in those days and there was no valid reason on the surface for my marriage arrangement to be cancelled. When it became obvious that the marriage was inevitable, I tried to bargain in some way for the services of Lucretia so that she could remain by my side. This was not to be. Father and mother said her services were still needed to instruct my brother.

"Having been impressed throughout childhood of the responsibilities as well as the privileges of the aristocracy, I dutifully prepared to fulfill my new role as wife to the son of a nobleman. It was not an easy transition. To be perfectly frank, Joseph, I never did adjust to it. I gave it a noble try, if you'll pardon the pun, but I never even came close to overcoming my basic instinctive desires to relate sexually to females.

"The thought of a lifetime of sexual relations with my husband-to-be was frightening and almost repugnant to me. I admit to a certain curiosity at the time, but my overall feeling was one of antipathy. Deep rumblings within me kept screaming out that this was not natural for me to be making love to a man.

"Not only was it my destiny to remain the good wife in that life, but it was also in my life plan to become a mother. The traumas of a lesbian play-acting the role of the dutiful wife were endless. The traumas of impending and actual motherhood were legion. The thought of breast feeding, for instance, while not actually repulsive to me, was almost totally alien to my innermost instinctive feelings and drives.

"I cannot begin to recall or recount to you the enormity or the sum total of frustrations, anguish, mental and emotional turmoil and agony, anxieties and feelings of loneliness and guilt in that life. And yet, I was extremely fortunate. My husband was a kind and good man. He was thoughtful, considerate and generous. Without those qualities, I would have considered my situation hopeless. He never suspected that I had intimate longings and desires beyond his capacity to fulfill.

"I never did find another confidante in that life to replace Lucretia. Until the day I died, my lesbianism remained a mystery to me," Diane concluded.

CHAPTER 21

"While Diane is gathering her thoughts as to how to condense her last five lifetimes, Joseph, I will relate to you some highlights of the life I spent in England in the twelfth century," said Michael. "Perhaps you may recall that was the time of the Christian Crusades. My father was a serf to one of the Christian Barons. The life of a serf was probably never an easy one in any country or any era. It is for certain it was not easy in England at that time. You might reasonably assume that to be the serf of a Christian Baron was certainly preferable to being the serf to a pagan one. That was not necessarily the case. The Baron that ruled us was fanatical to the point of harshness in his religious zeal. He most certainly was not influenced by his heart in matters of doctrinal interpretation. He could best be described as a rather strict letter of the law person.

"My father was what might be termed the head serf. He was something like a foreman, though with none of the privileges or rewards that one might expect a foreman to enjoy. Serfs were not accorded such benefits. He was treated with more respect than were the other serfs because of his greater intelligence and ability, and because his influence over the other serfs was very useful to the Baron.

"I was second oldest of three sons. My name was Raymond. The only happy memories I have of that life were the years from about three to five. It was the only carefree time I ever had. It was the only time when my mind and emotions were not filled with irreconcilable conflicts. Yet the only happiness I had even then was when I was alone in the fields and woods with the little beings that inhabit the woodlands and forests. My only friends were the animals and birds, along with the fairies, leprechauns and other elemental beings thought not to exist by most people.

"My oldest brother picked on me constantly whenever we were together. My younger brother was the family pet. I always felt like a nobody. To compound my misery, I didn't feel like I thought a little boy was supposed to feel. The games and roughness of little boys shocked and upset me. I wanted to play with little girls instead but the rules of that culture ostracized me from such participation. As a result, I had no one to play with and my loneliness grew.

"From about the age of six, my life was filled with enough chores to keep two people busy. My mother was the only one in my family with whom I could relate at all. Still, I could not get close to her because she seemed ashamed of me. As for my father, he treated me as though I didn't even exist. As I approached my teen years, my body had grown reasonably strong because of all the work I did. Nevertheless, I was no match physically for most other boys my age. My heart was not in their roughhousing ways.

"When puberty began to announce its hirsute presence,

I did not know how to react. At that point, I had no rapport with anyone. I was alone in every sense of the word except physically. I had no close friend or confidant. I was excluded from most group activities of either the boys or the girls. Perhaps you would say that it was fate that intervened to change my life's direction just when I was most confused and lacking guidance.

"While alone in the forest one day with my frustration and bewilderment, I heard a horseman approaching at a canter in my direction. I was sitting astride a branch of a large tree directly above the trail. While still a hundred feet away, the horseman glanced upward and saw me before I could hide. He stopped at the base of the tree while I cringed apprehensively above. He was a young man in his very early twenties and I recognized him as one of the sons of the Baron. After a few moments, he asked me what I was doing and my name. When I replied, he told me to come down from the tree. As I climbed down, he dismounted. Taking the reins in his hand, he began leading his horse off the trail and told me to follow him. We walked for several minutes, then he stopped and tied the reins to a small tree and told me to sit down. Sitting facing me, he told me his name was Bruce and then he asked me if I knew who he was. I told him that I had seen him before a number of times and that I thought he was the Baron's son. He then told me that he had already known who I was. He said that he had first noticed me about two years before and that he had been observing me grow up since then. He asked me if I wanted to work for him personally as his page. My heart almost leaped from my chest at his offer.

"One of the greatest dreams of any serf boy was to have the opportunity to be a page to anyone of the ruling class. I could not believe what I was hearing. Such good fortune could not possibly happen to me. Before I even knew what was expected of me, I answered yes. Only one who has lived as a serf can relate to the elation I felt at the prospect of leaving that life. Only one who has lived a life of rejection can appreciate the joy I felt that at last someone wanted me. That day I had no basis in understanding or experience to wonder why Bruce had been attracted to me. It would not take me long to find out.

"I was almost completely naive. The rejection which had been forced upon me because of my slightly effeminate bearing had prevented me from learning what most kids discover by age twelve or thirteen. I knew nothing about sex except what I had observed in the barnyard. I had by that time been experiencing wet dreams for about six months. Although the dreams provided me with tremendous physical pleasure, they also terrified me because I didn't know what was happening or why. Besides, I didn't actually dream anything insofar as sexual intercourse or masturbation. In my dreams, I would simply have an erection, and the moment I would grasp my penis in my hand in my dream, I would then experience the ejaculation. It did not occur to me that I could enjoy the same experience while awake.

"When I agreed to become his page, Bruce immediately took me back to my parent's hovel to inform them. While it was an honor for them to have their son and brother chosen for such a position, they were still jealous and angry at losing my services. Joy did not shine in their faces, but I could not hide my own jubilation. That was the last I saw of them.

"Bruce then took me to the manor house and gave

me a place to sleep in the barn. The accommodations
were far superior to any I had ever known, which should
give you some idea of the average lifestyle of a serf. I
also received new clothes and my first shoes befitting a
page of the Baron's son. If I was ever what you would
call happy in that life, it was during this brief span of
time. Bruce was stern with me, but he was also kind in
his own way and he quickly showed me what was expected
of me in my duties and in our interrelationship. He lost
no time in finding out what I knew about sex, then he
proceeded to teach me what he wanted me to know to
give him pleasure. Basically, he and I were the same in
our propensity towards homosexuality so I really did not
feel any revulsion towards him. Outwardly, he did not
betray his inner preferences by any effeminate manner-
isms. Insofar as my own deepest inner feelings were concerned at the time, I enjoyed our relationship. To me it
felt perfectly natural to make love to a man. Frankly, I
would have been terrified at the thought of making love
to a female.

"I had been Bruce's page for several months when he
told me that we would soon be leaving for a very, very
long journey. The Baron had decided to join forces with
two other Barons on a Crusade to recover the Holy Lands
from the Muslims. Word had reached the Baron of a
new gathering taking place in what is now France to finally
wrest control of the Holy Lands from what they considered heathens. None of the previous crusades had been
successful because the journey was so long, the hardships
so great and the enemy so strong and clever. Only opti-
mism born of ignorance could have persuaded them that
this crusade would be different.

"I cannot begin to tell you the hardships we were forced

to endure. What had begun as an heroic adventure for God turned into a nightmare that violated every precept which the God-loving adhere to. As weeks turned into months on the trek across Southern Europe, I daily witnessed the pillage and rape of a misdirected quest. While disease and starvation thinned our ranks, many of the survivors committed the most heinous acts imaginable in the name of God. If I had not been a page to the Baron's son, I would not have survived as long as I did. Believe me, I often wished for death to relieve me from the hardships. Finally death did intervene, and the land of spirit never beckoned so sweetly.

"That was my first lifetime as a homosexual. From the realm of spirit I undertook to appraise that short life span of fourteen years to determine the lessons I had learned for eternity. The first and most obvious lesson was to experience and understand the degree of isolation that is forced upon those who differ from the arbitrary norms imposed by their culture. Almost equally important was the lesson to be discovered from the daily struggle of dealing with basic impulses and urges which could neither be understood nor ignored. Although I knew before I incarnated that I was going to be faced with the dilemma of homosexuality, I did not have the solace of this remembrance during the incarnation. Very high on the list of lessons learned was tolerance. Can one who has never been harshly discriminated against fully comprehend the need for tolerance?

"The most important lesson of that life was to feel what it was like to go through a whole lifetime without love. Fortunately, it was a short life. Even so, for one whose basic nature was one of love, to go through even a portion of one's life without love was desolate and traumatic. The closest I came to any experience of love was my relationship with Bruce. Yet I knew in my heart that he felt absolutely nothing for me. He thought of me only as an object.

"I was greatly relieved to have completed my first episode into the transitional life of the homosexual.

CHAPTER 22

"In the land of spirit, Diane and I are the closest of friends. Just as Cassandra and Hector have always done, we have assisted each other as much as possible in our respective evolutionary paths. After each physical incarnation, we have counseled together to assess our growth and understand the lessons we have learned.

"After my life as Raymond, I could comprehend much better the traumas Diane had experienced as Paphia. Although a thousand years separated our respective incarnations, this is of no significance in the spirit worlds. We compared the hardships, frustrations and difficulties we had each endured and we concluded that Raymond had a far more difficult time although his life was of a shorter duration. To live any life without love automatically makes such a life more arduous. Paphia's life, though frustrating, was filled with many of the mundane advantages that take away the sharp edges from the pain of living. In addition to that, love was not a stranger in her life. By contrast, the only blessings in Raymond's life were its brevity and the harsh lessons learned."

Pause.

"Joseph, Diane and I have decided that it is not necessary to the substance of our story to go into any further

211

specific detail concerning our subsequent physical incarnations. In summing up our remarks about these lifetimes we will simply speak in a general way, and as one.

"We had known from the land of spirit that we would be faced with many inescapable dilemmas in experiencing a number of lives with homosexual tendencies. We also knew that it was unavoidable. From our own vast experience and observation, we knew that it would be necessary for us to build up a storehouse of memories and habit patterns to counterbalance our homosexual tendencies in our physical bodies. We planned each lifetime very carefully so that we could hopefully offset the tremendous sexual and emotional impulses that were driving us in the opposite direction from the gender of our physical bodies. For a long time, we observed from the land of spirit the many problems that confronted homosexuals in the various cultures in the physical world. This helped us to program and prepare for our Earth lives in such a way as to accelerate the transition we were going through.

"Due to our extensive planning and preparation and to the invaluable assistance of our many friends in spirit, we were each able to reach a point of balance in our respective last lifetimes. It was these last lives in which we were known as Michael and Diane. We only just completed those lives in your twentieth century. The things and lessons we have learned are urgently needed in your world at this time. Time nears an end and there is still much ignorance to be overcome in order for man to make intelligent choices among his options.

"Psychiatrists and psychologists, priests and rabbis, educators and counselors are all perplexed by homosexuality, and always have been. It's time to dispel some of the ignorance that surrounds this phenomenon and place things in their proper perspective. It's time to erase the guilt from the minds of those homosexuals upon whom society has placed the impossible burden of perversion. It's time to place the lie to those homosexuals who flaunt their proclivity as the highest estate of man. Homosexuality is, purely and simply, an unresolved habit pattern. Once homosexuals truly understand the reasons behind their propensity, then they can intelligently modify their life style to conform with their eternal goals.

"This was the struggle in which we found ourselves whenever we incarnated into the physical body. Our sexual preferences usually made us feel isolated and lonely. Until our final life, we always felt like we were abnormal, like freaks. Even though in each homosexual life, we always managed to meet others like ourselves, it was never free of the guilt and onerousness which society imposes. It was in the lifetime preceding our final lifetime that we finally managed to reach that point of understanding that allowed us to turn the corner in our soul evolution and growth. It was in that lifetime that we both met a great teacher who at last was able to teach us how and why to modify our habit patterns to conform with our physical gender! This great teacher taught us how habits are formed and how they can be restructured. He told us about the reality of reincarnation and about the stranglehold which past-life habits exert upon any given lifetime! He illustrated to us that such past-life habits are the most insidious, the most difficult to recognize and change.

"He explained to us the factors that enter into the formation of a habit. Whether one is speaking of habits of mind, body or soul, habit formation is governed by the same ingredients. The basic components that contribute to the actual formation of a habit are repetition, emotion and the interplay of the conscious and subconscious minds. Naturally, whenever a habit involves the physical body in any way, there is also the physiologic component. However, when we refer to habits that involve the physical body, we are not speaking of physiologic aberrations produced by various kinds of chemical addictions and alterations. We are speaking only of learned body responses involving repetition, emotion and mental control.

"You could compare the formation of a habit to the making of a videotape which is etched into both the physical brain and into the subconscious, non-physical brain. Modes of behavior acquired through habit formation are similar to the automatic replaying of the videotape and the mimicking of the recording through voluntary or involuntary bodily, mental and emotional responses. In order to change a habit, one has to change the existing recording by replacing it with the desired new habit pattern. Death of the physical body does not in any way destroy the accumulated videotaped habits of a lifetime. These patterns follow us intact into the world of spirit. Whenever we reincarnate, these accumulated videotapes of all previous lifetimes are still attached to us. They are locked into our subconscious minds. There they will stay until the day that the conscious mind becomes aware of them and proceeds to restructure them.

"The videotaped habit patterns which are acquired in the physical incarnations, cannot be changed in the spirit worlds. They can only be dealt with, changed or modified while in the physical body. This is the great secret of acquiring mastery of the physical dimensions. Once we became fully aware of this process, Diane and I set about adjusting our life styles to accommodate the new habits we chose to acquire.

"This great and illumined teacher explained to us that we would keep returning and returning as homosexuals until we finally learned to express the natural characteristics which were inherent in the gender of the physical body we had chosen. Since neither Diane nor I had the slightest need or desire to experience another homosexual life, we resolved to make every effort to change and modify our sexual, emotional and mental habit patterns in that particular life. I am happy to report to you that we succeeded.

"We did not totally eliminate every vestige of our conflicting emotional-sexual tendencies. There were still lingering reminders in many little areas of our consciousnesses. However, we did master most of the large and difficult areas. We did so well that when we reincarnated the last time, we were able to live what you would call normal, happy and productive lives. We did so well, in fact, that our consciousnesses reached heights never before attained by us in the Earth.

"As unbelievable as this may sound to you, Joseph, Diane and I were both able to attain the level of the cosmic sexual experience. This only goes to prove how far one can progress in a single lifetime. Here is how it happened.

"In our lifetime when the great teacher helped us to balance our goals and objectives, Diane and I became good friends. Our teacher had introduced us. Through his encouragement we had learned how to work together to rearrange our habit patterns. In our last lifetime as Michael and Diane, we met each other shortly after we both had divorced our first mates. If ever there was an example of love at first sight, it occurred the moment Diane and I gazed into each other's eyes! From that moment on, there was never an instance when a direct gaze did not paralyze both of us with love and excitement.

"We did not concern ourselves with the rituals of conventional marriage. In our way of thinking, feeling and relating, we did not believe that type of formality was required to join us. We soon began to feel as if we had always been together. Our attitude towards each other was one of total mutual love, respect and support. The sense of responsibility which we both displayed in our relationship was far greater evidence of our marriage than any exchange of vows before a third party. With this attitude, our love exchanges soon blossomed into incredibly moving and powerful unions. As was the case with Cassandra and Hector, we then began to experience altered states of consciousness. Without actually realizing what we were doing, we had been gradually increasing the length of our unions and we had been performing those other requisites which increase the speed of the electron movement within the atomic structure of our bodies.

"As our transcendent encounters grew in frequency and in clarity, we both began to experience glimpses into some of our past lives. The revelations exposed to us through these fleeting views began to startle us with their implications. Diane and I were beginning to see a large number of our past lives in which Diane was a man and I was a woman! In time, our most recent lives in which Diane was a woman and I was a man began to be revealed to our awareness.

"At last the full picture emerged. Diane and I had finally attained that state of being that marks the completion of the evolutionary process in the physical worlds. We had become androgenous. As you know, androgenous means that we had acquired the balanced characteristics of both the male and the female roles. Many people think that androgenous means that someone has finally reached a sexless state, a state of being in which sex is neither desired nor necessary. The exact opposite is true. To be androgenous means that one has finally reached a state of totally balanced sexuality. It means that one can express as either the male or the female polarity for a given lifetime, and do so in perfect balance. It does not mean that one switches sex roles within a given lifetime. To be androgenous is to be comfortable in whichever body you are wearing, male or female, and to live within the sexual framework intended for that body, expressing as neither bisexual nor homosexual, but rather as heterosexual. It means that at last one understands the full implications of the duality of life and how they, as individuals, relate to all life. It means that one finally knows who they are and what life is all about. It means that at last one can appreciate the full impact and meaning of the words, 'Love is the only reason to live at all'!

"I love you, Joseph, and I thank you for listening to our story," said Michael.

"I am Cassandra—Diane is Hector!"

"Man laughs at his greatness in taming the atom, but man has tamed nothing and man is only a fool. When man can tame the power of LOVE, then man has tampered with power!"
Proteus

EPILOGUE

To those perceptive readers who have discovered in this book something beyond an entertaining story, your attention is again directed to the following dialogues. Frequent rereading of these dialogues will open the floodgates of your soul memories and illuminate your consciousness with knowledge of profound universal truths which all religions have sought, but which none have yet delivered in their entirety.

1. The evolution of the soul, by The Great Archangel Michael, p. 18–19
2. The story of the ETERNALS, by The Great Archangel Michael, p. 20–29
3. Habit formation and the subconscious mind, by Michael, p. 56–58
4. The most important form of communication, by Michael, p. 78
5. The God potential of human beings, by Nova Eight, p. 93–96
6. The sexual nature of human beings, by Nova Eight, p. 97–102
7. The purpose of planets Earth and Reath, by Nestor, p. 109–110
8. The nuclear dynamics of cosmic sex, by Michael, p. 136–138

GLOSSARY

Achilles. Mythological identity—Son of Peleus and the sea goddess Thetis. Educated by the centaur Chiron. Greatest Greek warrior of the Trojan War. He killed Hector, the greatest Trojan warrior. Plot identity—Greatest Greek warrior, who killed Hector, the principal male character of this story.

Aeneas. Mythological identity—Son of the Trojan prince Anchises and the goddess Aphrodite. Great warrior in the Trojan War. Founded the Roman race in Italy. Plot identity—Assistant to Theseus in early Atlantis. Later reincarnated in Atlantis' prime, using the same name, Aeneas, and was the greatest engineer-builder in Poseid and also a member of the ruling council.

Aladran. Plot identity—The finest craftsman of quality garments in the ancient Lemurian city of Xanthia. Father of Ilus (Hector) and father-in-law of Naomi (Cassandra) in their first Earth incarnations. Later incarnated as the great ruler Cronus during Atlantis' prime.

Andromache. Mythological identity—Devoted and faithful wife of Hector and mother of Astyanax during time of Trojan War. Plot identity—Same as mythological identity. Andromache was Euterpe, the wife of Victor (Hector), in Atlantis.

Aphrodite.   Mythological identity—The goddess of love. One of the twelve Olympians. Daughter of Zeus and Dione. Mother of Aeneas. One of the most famous of the gods and goddesses, she loved laughter, beauty and pleasure. Plot identity—Wife of Ares, Ruler of Mars, she accompanied Ares to Earth to attend the wedding of Victor (Hector) and Euterpe in Ciudad de Oro.

Apollo.   Mythological identity—son of Zeus and Leto. One of the twelve Olympians. The sun god, and god of fine arts, music, poetry and medicine. Gave Cassandra the gift of prophecy during time of the Trojan War, but when Cassandra refused his advances, he effected a curse that no reliance would ever be placed on her predictions. Plot identity—Son of Aristaeus and Latona, brother of Cassandra and Artemis during Cassandra's major Atlantean lifetime. Devoted lover to Cassandra during time of Trojan War.

Arcas.   Mythological identity—Son of Zeus and Callisto. King of Arcadia (which was named for him). Plot identity— Husband of Melissa, father of Dionysus and Euterpe. Minister of Technology and master of agricultural science in the underground city of Ciudad de Oro during Atlantis' prime. Became the father-in-law of Cassandra and Victor (Hector) at that time.

Arcturus.   A giant fixed star of the first magnitude in the constellation Boötes in the Northern Hemisphere. It is the third brightest star (sun) of the Northern Hemisphere and the sixth brightest in our visible sky, with a magnitude of 0.2. According to the revelations in this story, Arcturus has three major planets revolving around it, and is the home world of the Novic people who control vast sectors of space.

Ares.   Mythological identity—God of War. One of the twelve Olympians. Son of Zeus and Hera. Illicit lover of Aphrodite. Plot identity—Ruler of Mars during time of Victor's (Hector) and Cassandra's major Atlantean incarnations. Visited Earth with his wife Aphrodite to attend the wedding of Victor (Hector) and Euterpe in Ciudad de Oro.

Aristaeus. Mythological identity—Son of Apollo and Cyrene. World traveler who settled in Greece. Married Autonoe, daughter of Cadmus. He was a keeper of bees, the inventor of bookkeeping and he learned to raise olives. Plot identity—Most renowned horticulturist in Earth during Atlantis' prime, rumored to have been fathered by a prince of godly lineage from the Constellation Musca. Husband of Latona, father to Cassandra, Apollo and Artemis during featured Atlantean incarnation, and father-in-law of Dionysus. World's greatest authority on bees and honey.

Artemis. Mythological identity—Daughter of Zeus by Leto (Latona). Twin sister of Apollo. The moon goddess and goddess of hunting. Plot identity—Daughter of Aristaeus and Latona, sister to Cassandra and twin of Apollo in featured Atlantean civilization.

Astyanax. Mythological identity—Son of Hector and Andromache during time of Trojan War. Plot identity—same.

Atlantis. Mythological identity—Continent and civilization that existed prior to currently known historical records. Like the ancient continent of Lemuria in the Pacific, most of the land mass of Atlantis now lies buried beneath the Atlantic Ocean. Plot identity—The greatest spiritual, cultural and technological civilization which the Earth has yet produced. Now, in the twentieth century, the reincarnated souls of the great Atlanteans are reinventing and recreating the marvelous achievements of the past. America is the focal point for this reemergence.

Berenice. Mythological identity—A woman very famous for her beauty who married her own brother. Plot identity—Wife of Nestor, ruler of the extraordinary planet, Reath.

Mother of Protogenia, during the time span of Atlantis' prime.

Bruce.   Plot identity—Homosexual young man who lived in England during the twelfth century. Had a relationship with Michael, who is telling this story, during the crusades.

Byrten.   Plot identity—Father of Cyntha (Cassandra) and husband of Rhea during the earliest days of Atlantean civilization. He was also Virga, a son of Aladran, in the Lemurian civilization.

Cassandra.   Mythological identity—Daughter of King Priam and Queen Hecuba of Troy during time of the Trojan War. Reputed to be the most beautiful woman of that day, with the possible exception of Helen of Sparta (also known as Helen of Troy). Plot identity—Cassandra, in her many Earth incarnations, is the principal female character of THE ETERNAL QUEST. We learn that the mythological account of her life in Troy is highly distorted.

Citadel.   The ethereal 'land' created by the Great Archangel Michael as the abode of the great souls. The Citadel later became known as Heaven. Heaven is a non-physical frequency that now exists in multiple locations throughout the creation. It is the most blissful, ecstatic and euphoric vibration that exists this side of Paradise (see Paradise).

Ciudad de Oro.   One of the greatest of the true wonders of the world. Ciudad de Oro is an immense interplanetary spacecraft hidden beneath the jungles in the center of South America. This craft is the true "City of Gold" referred to in the legends of some South American explorers in recent centuries.

Coeus.   Mythological identity—Son of Uranus and Gaea. Husband of Phoebe, father of Leto (Latona) and Asteria. One of the twelve Titans. Plot identity—Father of Latona (who was mother to Cassandra in her major Atlantean incarnation). Atlantean ruler who preceded Cronus.

Cronus. Mythological identity—The youngest son of Uranus and Gaea. One of the twelve Titans. Husband of Rhea. Cronus and Rhea were the parents of six of the twelve Olympians—Zeus, Hades, Poseidon, Demeter, Hera and Hestia. Plot identity—Father of Victor (Hector) during featured major Atlantean incarnation. Chairman of the governing council of Poseid. Husband of Rhea. Cronus was Aladran in Lemuria.

Cyntha. Plot identity—Name of Cassandra in her first incarnation in the civilization that later became known as Atlantis.

Diane. A great soul now in the world of spirit, who, along with Michael, is telling this story. Her true identity is revealed in the climactic ending of the story.

Dionysus. Mythological identity—The God of wine. He was the youngest of the twelve great Olympians. Known by the Romans as Bacchus. Son of Zeus and Semele. Plot identity—Husband of Cassandra during her great Atlantean incarnation. Son of Arcas and Melissa and brother of Euterpe in the great underground city, Ciudad de Oro. He succeeded Heracles as ruler of Ciudad de Oro.

Endymion. Mythological identity—A youth of surpassing beauty. Son of Zeus and Calyce. King of Elis. Plot identity—Minister of Education of the planet Reath.

ETERNALS. The true Gods of Antiquity whose subsequent human fragments became incarnated as the Titans and Olympians of mythology. They are twelve in number, including the Primal God. Adam and Eve (Adruum and Epsilon) were the first and second ETERNALS, respectively, to leave Paradise on the quest to end God's loneliness—THE ETERNAL QUEST.

Euterpe. Mythological identity—The muse of music and lyric poetry whose symbol was the flute. Associated with Dionysus and Apollo. Plot identity—Wife of Victor (Hector) during his major Atlantean incarnation. Daughter of Arcas and Melissa and sister of Dionysus.

Gabriel The Archangel. One of the twelve Archangels, each of whom is actually a multilevel identity of one of the twelve ETERNALS. The Primal God has frequently used Archangel Gabriel as a special messenger to mankind in time of need.

Great Blue Wall. There is no mythological reference to the Great Blue Wall. This term has been given by direct revelation to the Author of THE ETERNAL QUEST, and refers to that demarcation that separates Paradise from the Creation.

Hector. Mythological identity—Son of King Priam and Queen Hecuba of Troy during time of the great Trojan War. Husband of Andromache. Father of Astyanax. Hector was respected as the greatest and bravest of the Trojan warriors and was the captain of the Trojan forces. He was killed by the greatest of the Greek warriors, Achilles. Plot identity—Hector, in his many identities, is the principal male character of THE ETERNAL QUEST.

Hecuba. Mythological identity—Queen of Troy at the time of the Trojan War. Wife of King Priam. Mother of fifty sons and twelve daughters, including Cassandra and Hector. Plot identity—same.

Hilda. Plot identity—Wife of Theseus. Mother of Victor (Hector) during an early Atlantean incarnation.

Heracles. Mythological identity—Also known as Hercules. Son of Zeus and Alcmena. None in mythology have been more renowned for feats of strength. He was taught, trained and equipped by many of the Gods of antiquity. Plot identity—Great ruler of the underground city, Ciudad de Oro, during the time of the featured Atlantean incarnations of Cassandra and Victor (Hector). One of the wisest men of Earth.

Ilus. Mythological identity—Fourth king of Troy. At the time of his reign, Troy was then named Ilion in his honor. Ilus renamed the city Troy for Tros, his father, who gave his name to the Trojans. Plot identity—Hector's first Earth incarnation was as Ilus, son of Aladran in ancient Lemuria. His wife was Naomi (Cassandra). He was a highly skilled craftsman in the garment industry.

Iris. Mythological identity—Goddess of the rainbow. Messenger of the Gods. Plot identity—Youngest sister of Victor (Hector) in his first major Atlantean incarnation. She was the greatest oracle of her time. Older sister of Naomi (Cassandra) in Lemuria. Close friend of Cassandra during Cassandra's major Atlantean lifetime.

Janus. Mythological identity—Known as the God of good beginnings. The month of January is named for him. The most ancient king who reigned in Italy. Plot identity—A visitor to Atlantis from Earth's great underground city, Ciudad de Oro. He accompanied Cassandra to Ciudad de Oro during her major Atlantean lifetime.

Latona. Mythological identity—Also known as Leto. Daughter of the Titans Coeus and Phoebe. Mother of Apollo and Artemis. Plot identity—Wife of Aristaeus. Mother of Cassandra, Apollo and Artemis during Cassandra's major Atlantean lifetime.

Lemuria. Mythological identity—Ancient advanced Earth civilization in the Pacific Ocean that predated Atlantis. Also known as the lost continent of Mu. Plot identity—Same.

Lucretia. Mythological identity—The wife of Tarquinius, a king of Rome. Plot identity—Tutor to Diane (who is telling this story) during Diane's lifetime in 2nd century A.D. Italy.

Melissa. Mythological identity—One of the daughters of Melissus, King of Crete. Collector of honey. Plot identity— Minister of Agriculture and Horticulture of the great underground city, Ciudad de Oro, during the time of Cassandra's major Atlantean lifetime. Wife of Arcas and mother of Dionysus and Euterpe. Mother-in-law of Cassandra and Victor (Hector).

Michael The Archangel. One of the twelve Archangels. Also one of the ETERNALS, he was the last ETERNAL to leave Paradise. He intervenes in the affairs of man on behalf of God whenever required to ensure the inviolability of the Divine Plan of God. He created the Citadel, which in recent ages became known as Heaven. When necessary, he exercises the power of Love over those who misuse the love of power.

Michael. Along with Diane, the teller of this story. His true identity is revealed in the dramatic ending of the story.

Minerva. Mythological identity—Roman name for Athena. One of the twelve Olympians. Daughter of Zeus and his favorite child. Born from Zeus' head without a mother. Protector of civilized life, of handicrafts and agriculture. Plot identity—Mother of Naorni (Cassandra) and Iris in Lemuria. Daughter of Theseus and Hilda, sister to Victor (Hector) and Iris, and Aunt of Regina (Cassandra) in early Atlantis.

Naomi. Plot identity—First Earth incarnation of Cassandra, she was born in the great city of Xanthia in the ancient civilization of Lemuria 91,000 years ago.

Nestor. Mythological identity—The oldest and wisest of Greek chieftains at the time of the Trojan War. Son of Neleus and Chloris. The only one of twelve brothers not killed by Heracles. Plot identity—Ruler of Planet Reath during the time of the featured Atlantean incarnations of Cassandra and Victor (Hector). Husband of Berenice. Father of Protogenia.

Nova Eight. Plot identity—Minister of Education of the Novic people of the three planet system of Arcturus.

Olympians. Mythological identity—The twelve great Gods who succeeded the Titans. The term Olympians derives from the reputed name of their home, Olympus. This was once thought to refer to Mt. Olympus in Northern Greece, but later it was realized it was a realm that existed above Earth, but beneath Heaven. The Olympians were the children of the Titans. The twelve Olympians, like many things historical or mythological, are controversial as to identity. Those most frequently identified as Olympians are the following named: the Greek name is listed first, with the Roman name in parentheses. 1. Zeus (Jupiter). 2. Hera (Juno). 3. Poseidon (Neptune). 4. Demeter (Ceres). 5. Apollo (Apollo). 6. Artemis (Diana). 7. Hephaestus (Vulcan). 8. Pallas Athena (Minerva). 9. Ares (Mars). 10. Aphrodite (Venus). 11. Hermes (Mercury). 12. Hestia (Vesta). 13. Pluto, Hades, or Thanatos (Orcus or Dis). 14. Dionysus (Bacchus, Bromius or Liber). Plot identity—While philosophers have suggested various theories to explain the birth of mythological stories, THE ETERNAL QUEST strongly supports an historical basis, which states that most of the persons mentioned in mythology were once real human beings as well as god beings. They were, in fact, ETERNALS—or rather individualized fragments of the ETERNALS. As with most history, there have been ample additions and embellishments to the stories. That is why we have listed fourteen names instead of twelve. The alterations of the past have rendered agreement among most scholars unlikely, if not impossible.

Paphia. Mythological identity—A name for Aphrodite, the goddess of love, and one of the twelve Olympians. Plot identity—a lifetime of Diane (who is telling this story, along with Michael, from the world of spirit) in the 2nd century, A.D., in Italy.

Paradise. The birthplace and eternal home of the Gods. It is a place beyond Heaven or any other creation. It lies beyond the Great Blue Wall. God refers to Paradise as Home World, and promises its glories to all who attain Godhood through THE ETERNAL QUEST.

Phoebe. Mythological identity—Another name for Artemis, the moon goddess. Wife of Coeus. Plot identity—Wife of Coeus. Mother of Latona and grandmother of Cassandra, Apollo and Artemis in featured Atlantean incarnation of Cassandra. She was one of the twelve Titans.

Poseid. The oldest, largest and greatest city of the Atlantean civilization. It was located on what is now the southeastern coast of the State of Florida and it included the area of what is now Palm Beach.

Priam. Mythological identity—Last king of Troy. Husband of Hecuba. Father of fifty sons and twelve daughters (by Hecuba), including Cassandra and Hector. Plot identity—Same.

Prime Nova. The great ruler of all the Novic people and of countless other physical worlds as well. He still lives and is now over 50,000 years old. The Novic people live in the three planet system of Arcturus. These beings have long since conquered space and time. Though originally warlike, they now promote peace and the Divine Plan throughout the Universes. With his vast space armada, Prime Nova protects Earth and other key planets and sectors from destruction by the negative forces.

Protogenia. Mythological identity—The only daughter of Deucalion (Noah of mythology) and Pyrrha. Plot identity—Daughter of Nestor and Berenice on the Planet Reath. Victor's (Hector) lover during his interplanetary journey to the Planet Reath in the time of his major Atlantean incarnation. As Victoria, she was Victor's (Hector) wife during Victor's first Atlantean lifetime.

Raymond. Plot identity—A lifetime of Michael (who, along with Diane, is telling this story) in England in the twelfth century A.D.

Reath. The most highly evolved physical planet in the Creation. It is the idealized version of what Earth is to become upon the completion of the Divine Plan.

Regina. Plot identity—An early Atlantean incarnation of Cassandra. Daughter of Victor (Hector) and Victoria. Granddaughter of Cyntha (therefore she was her own granddaughter).

Rhea. Mythological identity—A daughter of Uranus and Gaea. She was called the 'Mother of the Gods'. Mother of Zeus, Poseidon, Hades, Demeter, Hera and Hestia. Sister and wife of Cronus. Plot identity—Wife of Aladran (Cronus) and mother of Ilus (Hector) and Virga in Lemuria. Mother of Cyntha (Cassandra) and wife of Byrten in Cassandra's first Atlantean incarnation. Wife of Cronus and mother of Victor (Hector) during Hector's major Atlantean incarnation. She was one of the twelve Titans.

Themis. Mythological identity—Daughter of Uranus and Gaea. One of the twelve Titans. First goddess to whom temples were built on Earth. Plot identity—A sea captain in Lemuria who delivered soft goods to Aladran. Husband of Cyntha (Cassandra) during her first Atlantean incarnation and a boat builder.

Theseus. Mythological identity—Son of Aegeus and Aethra. The great hero of the Athenians and one of their kings, he was also one of the most celebrated heroes of antiquity.

Plot identity—Husband of Hilda and father of Victor (Hector) in early Atlantis. A very astute and knowledgeable man, he became the most respected and powerful man in Poseid in his time.

Titans.   Mythological identity—The twelve great Gods of the first race. The children of Uranus (Heaven) and Gaea (Earth). Parents of the Olympians. Although there is no common agreement, many mythologists believe there were six males (gods) and six females (goddesses). The gods were 1. Oceanus. 2. Hyperion. 3. Crius. 4. Coeus. 5. Cronus. 6. Iapetus. The goddesses were 1. Tethys. 2. Thia. 3. Eurybia (Mnemosyne). 4. Phoebe. 5. Rhea. 6. Themis. The attributes of both the gods and the goddesses in order as their names appear were as follows: 1. sea. 2. sun. 3. memory. 4. moon. 5. harvests. 6. justice. Plot identity—As is the case with the Olympians, THE ETERNAL QUEST avers that the Titans were also human embodiments of the ETERNALS. The Titans were the ETERNALS' first human embodiments and the Olympians were their subsequent human incarnations.

Victor.   Mythological identity—A name used by the Romans referring to such gods as Hercules (Heracles), Mars, Jupiter and others. Plot identity—Hector's first Atlantean incarnation was as Victor, son of Theseus and Hilda, and brother of Minerva and Iris. In that life he married Victoria (Protogenia) and fathered Regina (Cassandra). Hector also used the name Victor in his major Atlantean incarnation as the son of Cronus and Rhea when he became ruler of Poseid.

Victoria.   Mythological identity—Roman name for Nice, Nike (Greek). The goddess of victory, greatly honored by the Greeks. Plot identity—Wife of Victor (Hector) and mother of Regina (Cassandra) in early Atlantis. Later incarnated as Protogenia, daughter of Nestor and Berenice on the planet Reath. Victor's lover when he visited Reath.

Virga. Plot identity—A son of Aladran in the city of Xanthia in ancient Lemuria. In earliest Atlantean incarnation, he was known as Byrten. Husband of Rhea and father of Cyntha (Cassandra). He built the first loom in Atlantis which his daughter Cyntha had reinvented.

Xanthia. Greatest city of the ancient civilization of Lemuria, which predated Atlantis. This was the city where Cassandra and Hector had their first human physical incarnation. They were known in that life as Naomi and Ilus.